THE VAMPIRE;

OR,

DETECTIVE BRAND'S GREATEST CASE

THE VAMPIRE;

OR,

DETECTIVE BRAND'S GREATEST CASE

By the author of "Star", "Harley Mayne" *etc.*

Illustrated by **JEREMY RAY**

AMERICA'S FIRST VAMPIRE NOVEL
AND THE SUPERNATURAL AS ARTIFICE

By **GARY D. RHODES** *and*
JOHN EDGAR BROWNING

ISBN 978-1-7363866-4-4
Library of Congress Control Number: 2021920347
Layout editor: Jana Horvath

Strangers From Nowhere Press
Chicago, IL
www.strangersfromnowhere.com

ABOUT THE BOOK

The Vampire; or, Detective Brand's Greatest Case was published on September 14, 1885, by the Munro's Publishing House, as No. 161 of their Old Cap Collier Library series. It was a dime novel: printed on cheap pulp paper, it cost 10 cents to purchase, and promised to be a quick, adventure-filled, and entertaining read. Dime novels were, up to that point, the most popular form of printed entertainment in the United States.

The Vampire has a rather intriguing premise: Detective Brand is asked to investigate a series of mysterious murders in New York City, where the victims are found with curious wounds on their necks, almost as if they were bitten by an animal... or a creature that only those seasoned sailors who traveled the Old World still believe in.

By 1885, American audiences were already familiar with tales of vampires — both in print and on the stage — but until that time, books about them were all European imports. In contrast with that, The Vampire is a truly American tale, unfolding on the familiar streets of New York City... and offering a rare glimpse of vampire lore that predates Bram Stoker's *Dracula*.

We are excited to introduce this forgotten gem of horror history to today's audiences, bringing it back to print for the first time since the nineteenth century. Our edition features illustrations by comic book artist Jeremy Ray, and a comprehensive essay by horror historians Gary D. Rhodes and John Edgar Browning, titled *America's First Vampire Novel and the Supernatural as Artifice.*

ABOUT THE AUTHOR

Unfortunately, as was common with dime novels, *The Vampire* was published without naming its author. The closest thing it offers to a credit is a line on the cover that reads:

> *By the Author of "Star", "Harley Mayne," etc.*

The aforementioned *Harley Mayne* was published as No. 141 in the series, with the full title *Harley Mayne, The Washington Detective; or, "Piping" A Mystery Of The Capital,* and only states that it was *By the Author of "Star," ETC., ETC.*

Star, The Expert Detective; or, On Track Of A Terrible Crime was released as No. 108. in the Old Cap Collier Library, and while it is also without a proper credit, from its cover we learn that it was written *By the Author of "The Scotland Yard Detective."*

This takes us to *The Scotland Yard Detective; or, "Piping" the Bunbury Mystery,* which was released on September 10, 1883, No. 36 in the series. Here, we are finally given the name of an author: Hawley Smart.

As the reader can see, it takes quite a few steps to arrive here, and we can't dismiss the possibility that a dime novel publisher simply highlighted other titles on their book covers as a form of advertisement. But even with that in mind, this breadcrumb-trail of credits makes Captain Hawley Smart (1833-1893), a British army officer turned novelist a likely candidate to be the author of *The Vampire.*

PRICE 10 CENTS.

Old Cap Collier

LIBRARY

Vol. 2. No. 161. Sep. 14, 1885. Subscription $10.

Entered at the Post-Office, N. Y., as Second Class Matter.

☞ Old Cap. Collier Library is Issued Semi-Weekly

THE VAMPIRE;

OR,

19053 2

DETECTIVE BRAND'S GREATEST CASE.

BY THE AUTHOR OF "STAR," "HARLEY MAYNE," ETC.

COPYRIGHTED, 1885, BY NORMAN L. MUNRO.

NEW YORK:
NORMAN L. MUNRO, PUBLISHER,
24 AND 26 VANDEWATER ST.

The original cover of The Vampire;

THE VAMPIRE;

OR,

DETECTIVE BRAND'S GREATEST CASE

BY THE AUTHOR OF "STAR," "HARLEY MAYNE," ETC.

CHAPTER I.

GOTHAM was puzzled.

The best detectives were at a loss, and candidly confessed their confusion. A serious of mysterious deaths and disappearances had called forth the best talent of the metropolitan detective force,- but as yet no substantial clew to the perpetrator of the awful murders, and mysterious disappearances, both believed to be the work of the same inhuman fiend, had been obtained. Murders were common enough in New York, but there was an unusual factor in these of which we write, and it was a something so ghoulish, so horrible, so unnatural, that even the tried officers of the force spoke of the matter with whispering voices, and sometimes with a shudder of superstitious horror that could not be repressed.

It was early in the evening of a mild spring day, that a policeman strolled along the streets that surround the Battery, swinging his club and whistling softly to himself.

At such an early hour as the time of which we write the streets were almost deserted, and so it happened that the policeman was the first to discover a man lying prostrate in the carriage-way, and he immediately jumped to the conclusion that it was some immigrant, who had been taking a look at the wonderful sights of great Gotham, partaken of too much strong liquor, and, overcome by the potent fluid, had lain down in the street to sleep off the effects.

"Oh, murther! isn't that a timperance lecture for yees!" the officer exclaimed in a rich brogue, which betrayed his nativity.

"I'll be afther running him in, so as to give him a chance to pay for his night's lodging. Shure, five dollars is not bad for an illigant bed like that, patent pavement for a mattress, and the whole of the beautiful sky for a blanket."

But when the vigilant guardian of the night came nearer to the supposed sleeper, he saw that it was no immigrant, for the man was dressed in an excellent suit of dark clothes, fashionably cut, and from his appearance looked like a well-to do merchant. He was a tall, portly man, well advanced in years, with gray hair and a long beard of the same hue.

"Oh, ho! upon my life, this is no small fish!" muttered the policeman. "I'll get a carriage for him, send him to his house or hotel, and thin strike him whin he gits sober for tin dollars for me trouble. For 'I'm a dandy cop of the Broadway squad,'" he hummed as he came up to the man and knelt down by his side.

The song, though, died away quickly when he placed his hand upon the stranger's person for the purpose of rousing him, and peered into his face.

"Mother of Moses! if he isn't dead!" he cried, startled by the unexpected discovery.

The policeman was right; the man was dead and had apparently been for some time, for the body was perfectly cold.

"Phat the divil is this, any way? Phat kilt the man?" queried the officer. "Has there been foul play — is it a murther?"

But no signs of violence met his eyes; the face of the dead man was as calm and peaceful as though he was only asleep, and his clothing was not disarranged. Only one suspicious fact the officer noticed; there were no articles of jewelry visible; no watch-chain, no studs, although there were eyelet holes in the shirt bosom, which seemed to indicate that the man had been in the habit of wearing such things.

The policeman cast a rapid glance around, and then hastily examined the dead man's pockets, but his search was a fruitless one; there was absolutely nothing whatever in them.

"Bedad! some one has been here before me," the officer said. "That is suspicious! Be the powers! I believe the man was kilt by some murtherin' thaves, but who in the world did the job?"

And as he put the question, he looked wistfully around. He had not the slightest anticipation of seeing anything, and therefore was not at all prepared for the sight which for a moment froze him with horror.

When he had approached the motionless man there was not a living thing in sight. On the left hand rose the walls of Castle Garden and the low sheds appertaining thereto. In the center was the sea wall and beyond that the waters of the bay, whereon rode at anchor vessels of all nations. On the right was the pier of the Iron Steamboat Company, and the approach to this was partially blockaded by huge piles of freight, destined, evidently, for the Pennsylvania Railway's freight depot, which was the next pier beyond.

As the policeman raised his head he looked directly at the huge pile of freight, and by the boxes stood a figure strange enough to startle almost any one, as it appeared, framed against the moon. The officer, credulous and superstitious by nature, stared in alarm.

"Holy Moses! is it a man or a divil?" he cried.

It was no wonder that he asked the question, for at a distance the figure, though evidently that of a man, bore a striking resemblance to a huge bird, being attired entirely in black, wearing a long, old-fashioned circular cloak, and just as the officer caught sight of the man, he raised and stretched out his arms, and the cloak being thus extended, looked exactly like a pair of huge wings, and as the man wore, too, a small, soft hat, pulled in chapeau fashion down over his eyes, so that it came to a point in front, it gave his head the appearance of that of a bird of prey.

The officer rubbed his eyes as if to make sure he was awake. When he looked again the figure had disappeared.

"Bad 'cess to me!" he muttered, "if the baste didn't give me quite a turn! Upon me wourd, I would have taken me oath whin I first saw it that it was a divil; but thin who iver saw a divil like that? or a man a-galavanting round in sich a rig? Mebbe it was wan of thim frog-eating Frenchman — they do be afther making monkeys of thim selves."

Then dismissing the subject from his mind, he turned his attention to the dead man. He felt absolutely certain he had been robbed, but whether before or after death was a question. As far as he could see, there wasn't the least sign to indicate that the man had been the victim of foul play, and the officer came to the conclusion that the stranger had died a natural death, being attacked by some fatal stroke on that very spot, and some night prowlers had discovered the body and removed the valuables.

"Upon me conscience!" the officer murmured, after completing his examination. "It's mighty odd that I niver have the luck to pick up a boodle of this kind once in a while."

Then he proceeded to summon assistance; the body was removed and the coroner notified, and in due time the inquest held, and then came a startling discovery.

The man had been murdered!

Right over the heart was a stab wound, so slight that hardly a drop of blood had come from it. Inflicted evidently by a dagger whose blade was very little larger than a good-sized knitting-needle: but the wielder of this toy-like instrument of death had such an accurate knowledge of the human frame, and knew so well where to strike his blow, that the steel had penetrated right through the heart. And then, too, on the left side of the neck, right over the jugular vein and under the ear, were two little punctures, hardly large enough to be classed as wounds, and which looked exactly as if they had been made by the teeth of some small animal.

This was really a wonderful case, and yet in a great city like New York so many mysterious deaths are constantly happening that even this occurrence created but little wonder in the minds of the public at large.

The newspapers briefly reported and commented upon the affair — "Mysterious death, murder evidently. where were the police? body recognized, something ought to be done" — and then the next day the matter was supplemented by some new horror, and the busy folks of New York forgot all about it. There were some exceptions to this rule, however. There was a man who after the lapse of a few days came forward and identified the body. One of the representative men of the city, this gentleman, by name Juan Anchona, a retired merchant, one of the millionaires of Gotham. The dead man was his brother Jose, who had been engaged in business in Texas for some twenty years, and had come to New York on purpose to visit him, Juan, whom he had not seen for years.

The New Yorker had been advised by letter that his long-absent brother was on his way to the city, and when time passed on and he neither saw nor heard from him, he became alarmed, and some morbid impulse prompted him to visit the Morgue where the unclaimed dead bodies are kept on exhibition, and there he found the man he sought in the gray-bearded stranger.

CHAPTER II.

In the private office of the superintendent of the New York police, sat three men, who, from the nature of their position, were presented constantly to the public gaze.

One was the superintendent of police, another the mayor of New York, and the third the governor of the state.

The governor and mayor had just entered the office, and had been received in due form by the police official, who, upon seeing his visitors, instantly suspected that something important had occasioned their visit.

The mayor plunged at once into the subject.

"We have called upon you, superintendent, in relation to this mysterious death of Mr. Jose Anchona," he said.

"His brother, Juan Anchona, is one of my most intimate friends," the governor explained, "and I have promised to do all that I can to have the murderer, or murderers, of his brother brought to justice. He, himself, has not allowed the grass to grow under his feet in the matter. He has communicated with his brother's friends in Texas — he has no relatives there, being a bachelor — and has ascertained that when his brother started for New York he wore a heavy gold watch and chain, two valuable diamond studs, a diamond ring, and carried two or three hundred dollars in his pocket-book."

"None of which, if you remember, superintendent, were found upon his person," the mayor remarked.

"I remember, sir," replied the official. "In fact, there wasn't a single article of any description in his pockets. He had been completely stripped."

"What can be done, superintendent?" the governor asked. "Money in this case is no object, you know. Mr. Anchona is wealthy enough to be able to afford to spend a hundred thousand dollars to bring the assassins of his unfortunate brother to justice, and for the sake of the good name of the city which you watch over, Mr. Superintendent, you ought to use every possible means to detect and punish the perpetrators of such an atrocious crime."

"Yes, this affair comes right home to both the governor and myself," the mayor added, "for while Mr. Juan Anchona is one of the governor's oldest friends, he is also a neighbour of mine, and I have known and esteemed him for years."

"Your honor, I have been doing everything in my power to get at the authors of this crime." the superintendent replied, earnestly. "Not only because the mystery that surrounds the deed has excited my curiosity, and piqued me to action, but also for the reason that it is not the first time that this mysterious slayer has struck down his man right in the open street. This fact I have kept to myself, for it isn't any use to make such a thing public, for if the newspapers got hold of it they undoubtedly would make a great row about the matter, thereby put the assassin on his guard and so make the task more difficult for the detectives. Just listen to these notes which I have jotted down in my private book."

Then the chief procured his note-book and read aloud:

"No. 1. Lawrence Whittaker, English, elderly, a stranger, tourist, man of means, stopping at Brevoort House, found dead, January 5th,- four o'clock in the morning, in Ninth Street, near Washington Park, all valuables removed from person. No signs of violence apparent on body, at casual examination, but when stripped, death was found to have ensued from a wound made by a minute dagger piercing the heart. On the neck, too, under the left ear, were two punctures seemingly made by a small pair of teeth."

Simultaneously the governor and mayor uttered a cry of astonishment.

"The resemblance of that crime to this murder strikes you, I see," the superintendent remarked.

"All the circumstances are exactly the same, with the exception of the place where the body was found," the governor remarked.

"Yes, and the position in the street, too, right in the middle of the roadway, as if the man had been assaulted in crossing the street, yet after a careful consultation with some of the most expert surgeons in the city, one and all assured me that it would not be possible, one time out of a thousand, for a man to inflict such a wound as caused death in these cases, unless the victim stood perfectly quiet, and then, too, they were all of the opinion that the punctures in the neck were caused by the teeth of some small animal. Now, gentlemen, see how improbable it is that these tragedies occurring right in the public thoroughfares could take place without causing an alarm, even though at an hour when all the city is supposed to be asleep. But listen to the others." Then the official read his notes regarding three more cases, all alike in respect to the victims being elderly well-to-do men, strangers in the city, all killed by the same means, and all rifled of their valuables. One body was found in Madison Avenue, just above Madison Square, another in Wall Street, a few doors from Broadway, and the third on Fifth Avenue, within a stone's throw of the lower end of Central Park.

"You will perceive," the superintendent observed, when he had finished reading the notes, "that Mr. Jose Auchona is the fifth man who has fallen a victim to this notorious assassin: for that one man, and one man only perpetrated these deeds of horror I feel quite certain. Another thing I feel sure of, too, and that is, the murders were not committed in the places where the bodies were found. It is entirely beyond the bounds of probability for these murders to have been committed in such public places, even in the early hours of the morning, when darkness shrouds the city, without exciting attention. My theory is that the victims were all decoyed to some desolate spot, where, even if a struggle ensued, no alarm could be given, and there the deed was done."

"But, then, why should the assassin take the trouble to deposit the bodies in these public places?" the governor asked.

"That is one of the idiosyncrasies of crime," the chief answered. "I do not suppose, gentlemen, that you are aware of it, but I have a peculiar theory in regard to criminals, particularly those who commit great crimes. I think that all persons who sin against the laws of God and man are in a measure diseased in their minds, not exactly lunatics, you know, but people whose heads are not well balanced. Now, in these cases, after the murders were committed, it was necessary for the assassin to ge rid of the bodies; and let me tell you, gentlemen, that is no easy job in a big city like New York. Some of the most noted murders that the world has known have come to light through the attempt of the murderer to get rid of the remains of his victims. The depositing of the bodies in these public places is pure bravado, a defiance to the authorities. The author of these deeds is no common criminal,- but a man of brains who has turned his talents in a wrong direction; a monomaniac, in fact, for I cannot bring myself to believe that these murders are committed for the sole purpose of plunder, for I feel pretty well satisfied that in nearly all these cases, the victim's valuables could have been obtained without the robber being obliged to add murder to theft."

"The perpetrator of these mysterious murders is a sort of demon, then — a human fiend who kills for the pleasure of killing," the governor observed, thoughtfully.

"The idea seems rather far-fetched," the mayor remarked. "His honor" was noted for his practical ideas.

"Yes, your honor, that is very true; but there is an old saying, you know, that 'truth is stranger than fiction,' and I think it is quite safe to say that the imagination of man cannot conceive anything stranger than the acts that some persons will commit. Take the case of this mysterious assassin, for instance; why, the records of crime do not contain a stranger case; we must go back to the old story of the crimes of Margaret of Burgundy in 'La Tour de Nesle,' as told by Victor Hugo, or the tale of the vampire, who prolonged his miserable existence by stealing from his victims the remnant of life which in the course of nature they would have lived if their career had not been brought to an untimely end."

"The vampire, by Jove!" exclaims the governor, abruptly. "Of course the idea is absurd, but don't these mysterious murders appear like the work of just such a set of creatures, although I believe the vampire never took the trouble to drive a weapon through the heart of his victim."

"No, he bled them to death by biting them in the neck," the mayor remarked.

"The two little punctures in the neck of these victims would fill that bill," said the superintendent. His visitors stared at each other for a moment, then, looking at the official, shook their heads gravely.

"The idea is too steep for you to swallow, eh?" asked the chief.

"Oh, yes, the days of vampires have passed away," the governor observed.

"Yes, yes; you can't come any 'La Tour de Nesle' business on us in New York," declared the mayor.

"Well, gentlemen, I have got a clew, and I will leave it to you to say if it don't have the smack of a vampire about it." and then the superintendent related how, in prying into the circumstances of the murder, he had extracted from the bull-headed policeman an account of the strange-looking figure which he had seen near the scene of the tragedy, and which at first he had taken to be a huge bird, at the same time never suspecting that it had aught to do with the dead man.

"Gentlemen, that bird, as the Irishman called it, is the party we want," the police chief said in conclusion, "and I have put some of my best men on his track, and whether he be man, or devil, or vampire, I will bet a good round sum that before a month is over I will have him safely locked up!"

Satisfied with this assurance the visitors departed, wondering greatly over the strange affair.

CHAPTER III.

Two young men sat in a cozy smoking-room of a sumptuous mansion on one of the fashionable cross streets of Murray Hill, as a part of the city sacred to the golden kings of New York is often termed.

Strong contrast these two young men each to the other.

One was slender in build and short in stature, with an olive-tinged, foreign-looking face, peculiar eyes of uncertain hue, appearing gray at times and then dilating into jet black: hair as dark as the raven's wing, and curling in little crispy ringlets all over his head; the face was smoothly shaven and appeared effeminate, yet there were certain lines around the eyes and the thin-lipped, resolute mouth which contradicted the general appearance of the countenance.

This was the master of the mansion, Victor Lee, commonly called "the doctor," by his acquaintances from a tradition which said he had once studied for a doctor in foreign lands.

Lee was commonly supposed to be very wealthy, although really the world at large knew but little about him. He had only resided in New York about a year, but had not experienced any difficulty in gaining an *entree* into society, owing to the fact that he was well acquainted with some of the leading young men of the upper-ten, whom he had met abroad. His story, as told them in brief, was this:

Lee was the only scion of an old Creole family, which had taken root years ago in Louisiana. He had never said much about his family, but from the fact that they were rich enough to send him to foreign lands to study for a doctor, and always kept him in funds so that he was able to gratify his slightest wish, his associates judged that the Lees were wealthy, and when studying in Europe young Lee was, to use the language of his companions, "Satan's own boy!" The leader of all the students in mischief and dissipation, it was often predicted that if the young Southerner did not die of drink he would get in some brawl which would end fatally for him.

As a student, Lee easily held his own against his companions, for he was wonderfully gifted, and seemed to have the faculty of comprehending upon the instant what would cost another man hours of severe study. In fact, he was a genius, all admitted that, and as more than one of his masters said, "he will be a great man one of these days, if he don't throw away his opportunities."

All of a sudden, right in the midst of his college studies, Lee was called home by the death of his mother, and none of his companions saw or heard aught of him, until he appeared in New York. Then, in answer to their queries, he said all his relatives were dead, and being his own master, he had come to the only city in the New World worth living in to enjoy himself. From the style of the establishment which he set up, and the manner in which he conducted himself, it was apparent that he had plenty of money. He pursued no business, although often in jest he would declare that he was a better doctor than nine-tenths of those who won princely incomes by following that profession, and so among his associates he was generally termed "Doc" Lee.

His companion was called Morgan May, a medium-sized blonde youth, with a face which, although fair to look upon, a good judge of mankind would not have been apt to form a favorable impression of.

This young gentleman, although not wealthy, moved in good society, for he came of an old family and was the cousin and confidential man of business of one of the richest men in the city, Juan Anchona, the retired banker.

"What is the matter? you seem out of sorts," Lee queried, after his visitor was comfortably seated and had his cigar in working order.

"There has enough happened to put me out of humor," the other replied, sulkily. "And I think that if you knew what I know, you wouldn't be in a very good humor yourself."

"Unfold yourself, although I doubt the truth of your statement, for I have such a deuced good opinion of myself, that it would take a great deal to worry me."

"Lee, can I trust you?" cried the other, abruptly, and with a searching glance at the face of his host, who laughed at the inquiry.

"Well, as to that, Morgan, my dear boy, you ought to be the best judge. You know what you can say and I don't, but if there is any doubt in your mind about the matter, give yourself the benefit of it and do not speak."

"Hang it, Doc, you and I ought to be in the same boat in this matter!"

"Yes, but, old fellow, two men can't very well pull together unless they have faith in each other; that is, to achieve anything, I mean."

"Well, you have as deep an interest in the matter as myself, and if you don't go in with me, you are not the man

I take you for. All I ask is for you to keep silent about the matter if you don't see your way clear to join me."

"All right, I give you my word that I will be as silent as the grave, so fire away!"

"In the first place let me get at your position. If I understand your game you are anxious to marry Miss Anita Anchona, old Juan's daughter and his heiress."

"I suppose I may as well own to that soft impeachment, though I trust you will do me the justice to believe that it is not altogether because Anita is an heiress that I am attracted."

"Oh, certainly; I understand that, but at the same time the fact that she is an heiress is no objection."

"Old fellow, with my expensive habits it would be sheer folly for me to pretend that a rich wife would not be a desirable thing for me to acquire, and I will go still further, Morgan, and say that if Miss Anita had not been likely to come in for a good bit of money one of these days, it is not likely that I should have ever troubled my head about her, beautiful and attractive as she is."

"You know that the lady doesn't regard you with a favorable eye, and that if you win her consent it will be because she yields to her father's request."

"Oh, yes; she doesn't particularly fancy me, but then she isn't in love with any one else, and I believe that she never will be, and so is not so much averse to marrying me as, under other circumstances, she might be."

"Now then, I will come directly to the point. You know Straub, the lawyer?"

The other nodded.

"He is Anchona's adviser, and when the old gentleman announced at lunch to-day that Straub was coming to see him on important business, my curiosity was excited, and I determined to know what took place at the interview, for I will own frankly, I am deeply interested. I am about the only relative, with the exception of his daughter, that the old man has, and I have always understood that at his death I was to be well remembered.

"The lawyer came in reference to the old man's will, as I suspected; I managed to overhear every word of the conversation, and now, prepare to be astonished! Anita is not Anchona's daughter, but an adopted child, and at his death she is to receive only a small part of his fortune, and that so tied up that the interest alone will come to her; a few thousand dollars are left to me, also invested so that I cannot touch the principal, curse the old scoundrel; so you see he doesn't trust me after all these years!"

"Too bad," and Lee shook his head; but there was a look in his eyes which seemed to say that he did not wonder at it.

"And the rest of his fortune, his millions daily growing larger and larger, what do you suppose is to become of them?"

"I haven't an idea, unless like many another old man in his dotage he is going to make up for the sins of his youth by giving money to some charitable purpose."

"No, crossing from England to this country, on the seas at this present moment, an emigrant passenger, is a young girl, without parents, without a living relative in the world, as far as she knows; she is called Helena Porras; she is to be received by the old lawyer, who was charged with the task of bringing her to this country, Anchona providing the money. The girl thinks some friends of her dead father, moved by charity, have brought her over, and she comes here to earn her living. The lawyer is to find a place for her; she is to be put on probation, the fact being carefully concealed from her; Anchona is to keep careful watch of her, and if she comes up to his anticipations, she is to be his heiress."

"The deuce you say!" cried Lee, startled by this intelligence. "Why, what on earth put the idea into his head? What is the girl to him?"

"Nothing at all; she is an entire stranger; he has never even seen her. Why, Straub, who as a general rule is not in the least curious, was amazed at the strangeness of the affair, but Anchona said he had good reason for this action, and that in time he would explain."

"I'll bet a trifle that the old man means to marry the girl."

"My own idea, exactly, for he said she was a beauty, and splendidly educated."

"What steamer is she on?"

"The City of Chester, due here next Monday. Now then, if the old man likes the girl after she arrives, and carries out this idea, good-bye both to your hopes and mine."

"We must keep a watch on the parties; the stake is worth some little trickery."

"You will go in with me, then, to put a spoke in the old man's wheel?"

"O, yes, for I want Anita, and I want a fortune with her too. There are plenty of tools to be found in a city like this who for money will do anything. We will watch events, and when the time comes be prepared to interfere."

And so the compact was made; two strong men against an old man and an innocent young girl.

CHAPTER IV.

PROMPTLY upon the date that she was expected, the City of Chester made her appearance in New York Harbor; only, being detained somewhat by fogs, she arrived in the evening instead of the morning, and so she came to anchor off quarantine, at which the passengers grumbled loudly, for one and all were impatient to reach the shore.

But it was not to be, and they were forced to content themselves with gazing at the dark outlines of Staten Island, rising plainly visible in the bright moonlight.

Among the steerage passengers, leaning over the bulwarks, and looking at the distant lights, visible here and there upon the crest of Staten Island, was a young girl, who was so beautiful that she had attracted much attention during the voyage.

This was Helena Porras, the girl referred to by the two plotters in our last chapter.

In figure she was about the medium size, most exquisitely formed, and with a face of rare beauty, being pure Greek, a perfect oval, and lit up by as handsome a pair of great, brown eyes, as ever dwelt in a woman's head.

She was plainly dressed, yet very lady-like in appearance, quite reserved in her manners, and so different from the usual run of single young girls who cross the ocean to seek a new life, that all of the officers of the ship who came in contact with her unanimously agreed that she was far more fitted to shine in the cabin than any lady on board of the ship. All wondered that such a girl should be obliged to cross the ocean alone, and in the steerage; but she had such a quiet, dignified way, that no one cared to run the risk of offending her by questions.

The third officer, a good-looking, blue-eyed, blonde fellow, was especially interested in the girl, and late on this particular evening happening to come across her, still gazing over the stern bulwarks at the distant land, he plucked courage to say a few words.

They were almost alone on the deck, nearly all the passengers having gone below.

"It's a fine night, Miss Porras," he remarked, as he came up to where she stood, wrapped in dreamy meditation.

"Yes, very pleasant, Mr. Blakely."

The officer answered to the name of Dick Blakely.

"You will be glad enough to get on shore tomorrow, I suppose," he remarked.

"I shall not be very sorry, although the trip has been a pleasant one."

Blakely hesitated and fidgeted about in an awkward way for a moment, and then said:

"I hope you will not think me inquisitive, but I suppose you have friends on shore ready to meet you?"

"Friends," and there was a mournful tone in her voice as she spoke, and her eyes had a vacant look as she gazed upon the waste of waters; "yes, I suppose so, although as yet they are strangers to me."

"Oh, I thought it likely that you had relatives on this side of the water."

"I haven't a relative in the wide world that I know of, and I do not really think that any exist."

"All alone in the world?"

"Yes; although perhaps I ought not to say that. For these strangers who have caused me to come across the ocean are acting like true friends; and as I have not had many so far in my life, perhaps fate designs to make up for the past by providing me with plenty in the future."

"Well, Miss Porras, if you will allow me, I should like to be ranked among your friends in the time to come, although now I am merely an acquaintance. This is my last trip on the steamer. I am about to embark in business on shore in New York. This will be my address hereafter, and if at any time I can be of any assistance to you, I hope you will not neglect to call upon me," and he handed her a card.

She placed it in her pocket-book, thanking him for the offer, which, in her present condition, affected her more than she cared to manifest.

"Yes, I am tired of a roving life, and have determined to settle down," he said. "I have secured a good business opening, and I think the chances are that I shall prosper."

"I am sure I hope so," Miss Porras exclaimed, and this was no mere empty compliment; for the kindness of the young man had made a deep impression upon her, and her wish for his success was sincere.

"What land call you that, sar?" asked a rather harsh voice at the ear of Blakely; and turning, he beheld one of the steerage passengers, all muffled up in a long, old-fashioned cloak, and with a slouch hat pulled down over his ears. In addition to the cloak, he had a woolen comforter wrapped around neck just as though he was cold, although the air was balmy and spring-like, as became a pleasant May evening.

In person, the man was under the medium size, with a swarthy face, fringed by coarse black hair worn quite long; a stubby, brown-black beard covered his chin, and altogether he presented a brigand-like although picturesque appearance.

"That is Staten Island," responded Blakely, taking a good look at the man, for he did not remember ever having seen him before, which he thought as strange, for he had an excellent memory for faces, and rather prided himself upon the fact. Then, too, the face of the man was an odd one — a face that, once seen, would not be apt to be forgotten.

"Staten Island," remarked the man, in a reflective sort of way. "That is not ze New York, then?"

"No; the city lies farther up the bay. But you will excuse my curiosity, I trust. Where on earth have you kept yourself during this voyage? I do not remember to have seen you; but you are a passenger of course."

"Oh, no; I have just dropped from ze clouds!" responded the man with a laugh, speaking in a pleasant, flexible voice, now strangely at variance with his rough, uncouth appearance; and from the slight accent which there was to his speech, Blakely came to the conclusion that he was a foreigner — either a Frenchman or an Italian.

"By Jove! I must say I don't seem to remember you any more than if you did; and it's deuced odd, for we haven't a large passenger list this trip. and I didn't think there was a person on board of the ship whom I hadn't seen."

"Oh, you saw me often enough, sar, at ze beginning of ze trip, but after ze first day I was attacked by ze dreadful sea malady and sought ze seclusion which ze cabin grants, as your divine singers say in ze 'Pinafore.'"

The man was a gentleman, evidently, despite the fact that no one would have taken him to be one from his personal appearance; but, somehow, a strange doubt had seized upon Blakely; he felt a sudden and most decided aversion to the man, and he could not get the impression out of his mind that, notwithstanding the assertion to the contrary, be had never set eyes upon his face before.

"How may I call your name, sir?" he asked, plainly betraying by his face that he regarded the other with suspicion.

"Alphonse Beauclerc."

"You are a Frenchman, I presume?"

"A French Italian," responded the man, with that peculiar shrug of the shoulders so common to the Latin races. "French by descent and reared in Italy."

Blakely had watched the stranger with an earnest eye. and the more he saw of him the more convinced he became that he had never set eyes upon the man before. He was not a passenger, for if he had been Blakely knew that he most certainly would have seen him. How, then, was it that he came to be on board the steamer? He could not very well have dropped from the clouds, as he asserted, although it was possible that he could have gained access to the deck of the steamer by taking advantage of the darkness and coming alongside in a small boat; but then what game was the man up to that he should take such a course? There wasn't anything to be gained by so doing, as far as Blakely could see, and he finally came to the conclusion that the fellow was a stowaway; that is, he had stolen on board the steamer without a ticket before she left England, and had managed in some mysterious manner to conceal himself among the freight and live through the voyage. Such a thing had been done, but very rarely, for after a day or two in the dark hold the stowaways were generally glad to sneak out and throw themselves upon the mercy of the officers.

If the man was a stowaway he had apparently managed to endure the voyage as well as anybody on board, and Blakely's curiosity was so excited by this strange circumstance that he determined to go instantly and examine the passenger list, and see if any such name was registered as the man had given, but without any intention of working harm to the stranger; for as long as the voyage was ended, and he was on this side of the water, it didn't matter materially how he had managed to get across.

"I imagined that you were either a Frenchman or an Italian from the way you spoke," Blakely observed, and, with a remark about the beauty of the night, he sauntered away.

"How strange are these English-speaking people," the man in the cloak mused, speaking apparently to himself, and yet loud enough so the girl could hear every word. "He doubts my statement; he thinks that I have fallen from ze sky, or else risen out of ze sea, and, in order to satisfy himself, he has gone to examine ze passenger lists, so as to discover whether I have spoken as truth or not, and how disappointed he will be when he ascertains that I am right in my account and he is weak in ze head for harboring such an idea. Ah! this world! what a strange world it is, eh, mademoiselle? Think how we poor humans go through life ever on ze watch against each other!"

"Oh, I think you are wrong in your surmise," the girl replied, puzzled by the man's manner, and half suspecting that he was not quite right in his mind.

"No, no! I am correct, as sure as that light burns yonder on ze land!"

Helena looked in the direction indicated, and then the man suddenly threw his arms around her, pressed one hand over her mouth, and, with the other, applied a sponge saturated with some strange-smelling liquid to her nostrils. She was in the toils.

CHAPTER V.

HELENA PORRAS was so taken by surprise, so thoroughly helpless in the strong arms of her assailant, who seemed to be possessed of demoniac strength, that she could neither scream nor struggle before the strong liquid with which the sponge was saturated stole away her senses. Her brain whirled; there seemed to be a gigantic wheel revolving within her head, and then, all of a sudden, the wheel burst with a brilliant shower of sparks, and she sunk into insensibility.

The moment he discovered, by the limpness of the girl's form, that her senses were stupefied, the assailant carefully laid her upon the planks at his feet; the deck was deserted, and he had taken advantage of the favorable opportunity.

There was no time to be lost, though, and this the fellow knew right well; although the night was well on, some of the passengers or crew were likely to make their appearance at any moment.

After relieving himself of the incumbrance of the girl, he drew from beneath his cloak a stout rope, with a carefully made loop in one end. This he passed around the girl's body, and then, fastening the other end to one of the stern posts of the steamer, he carefully lowered the insensible girl into a small boat, which floated on the tide under the ship's stern, attached to the rudder.

The bay was like a sheet of glass, and the tide, just at its height, was at the slack-water period, so that the maneuver was not so difficult as it might have been under other circumstances.

When the insensible girl was safely deposited in the boat, with the agility of a sailor or an acrobat the man descended the rope hand over hand; drew out his knife and with a single slash severed it; and just at that moment the tide turned, and the flood which had filled up the inner bay, again sought the sea; the boat floated away from the steamer and headed toward Sandy Hook.

The craft, though a small one, was a regularly built keel-boat, well suited to stand rough weather, and fitted with a sail; and after adjusting the girl in a comfortable position forward, the adventurer proceeded to get the sail up.

"That cursed officer suspected that I was up to some game and had made up his mind to spoil it, but I was quicker about the work than he anticipated, and now let him interfere with me if he can!" he muttered.

Shaking the sail out, he turned around and defiantly shook his fist at the steamer as he took his place at the stern and with his other hand grasped the rudder.

A cry of alarm coming from the deck of the City of Chester answered his defiance.

Blakely had examined the passenger lists, and not finding any name upon them at all like Alphonse Beauclerc, had returned to the deck to force the stranger to an explanation; and when he arrived there, finding that it was deserted, his attention was attracted first to the rope and then to the boat drifting seaward, for the wind was light and the little craft had not yet felt the influence of the sail.

The boat was still near enough to enable the young man to recognize the figures in it, and when he saw the girl lying motionless in the forward part, and the dark figure of the stranger at the helm, he immediately comprehended the greater part of what had occurred.

"The scoundrel came on board by means of that boat!" he cried. "What a fool I was not to look over the stern when my suspicions became aroused! The girl seems to be insensible! What vile plot is this?"

And then in hot haste Blakely hurried to the captain of the steamer and related what had occured.

The indignation of that gentleman was unbounded.

"What!" he cried, "one of my passengers abducted from my very ship? If that isn't the coolest piece of rascality that

I think I ever heard of since I breathed the breath of life! Why, hang the fellow's assurance! These New York vessels will be trying to steal the steamer next from right under my feet. Get a boat out immediately and give chase; there's very little wind to-night, and the chances are good that you will be able to overtake the scoundrel! Take command of the boat, Mr, Blakely, and don't give up the chase until you have secured the rascal."

The young man, whose feelings were deeply interested on behalf of the girl, needed no second command, and at once hurried away.

The discipline enforced on board the City of Chester, was excellent, and in a remarkably short time an eight-oared boat was in the water, and Blakely was cheering his men on in the chase.

The sailors bent to the oars with hearty good will, for there was something exciting about such a pursuit, and then the boldness of the deed roused their curiosity, so that they were eager to come to close quarters with the scamp audacious enough to so defy the law.

Thanks to the delay occasioned by the mustering of the crew and putting the boat into the water, the unknown had managed to secure about a mile's start; but as the breeze was light, hardly strong enough to ruffle the surface of the water, for the eight-oared beat to overtake the raft, although the fugitive had the advantage of a sail, did not appear to be at all improbable.

"Give way with a will, men!" Blakely cried. "We'll soon be up to him unless the wind rises."

The oldest man in the boat, the bo'swain, a brawny, weather-beaten old salt, who pulled stroke, and whom the rest looked upon as an oracle, shook his head in a dubious sort of way as he glanced upward at the sky.

"A stern chase is a long chase, yer honor, and I'm mortally afeared that this hyar breeze is going be something more than a cat-paw. It's from the east'ard, and I have allers noticed in this hyar bay, that sich a wind a-springin' up at this hyar time, generally 'mounts to something."

"The fellow is putting straight to sea, just as if he meant to run for blue water, and he will surely never dare to do that in such a cockle-shell of a boat, for if the wind should come up to anything of a blow it would apt to play the mischief with him, except he's an old and experienced sailor, and from what I saw of him I should set him down for a land-lubber."

"Ay, ay, yer honor," said the old salt. "He's either an able-bodied seaman, or a regular greenhorn, or he wouldn't run afore the wind as he is doing; for I tell you what it is, year honor, if we don't have a big blow afore we are an hour older, then my name ain't Tom Egan."

Blakely took a look at the sky. The old man was right; already the clouds had commenced to gather, and to a sailor's eye there was ample evidence that a storm was impending.

"It is going to blow," the young man remarked. "Well, so much the better; we'll drive him right out of the bay, and when he gets into rough water he'll be obliged to go about; then if it does not come up too dark, so that he can slip by us, we may be able to overhaul him."

On they went, gaining rapidly on the other craft, until hardly more than a quarter of a mile separated the two. By this time they had got past the twin lights on the Highlands, and were about abreast of the lighthouse on the point of Sandy Hook.

Before them lay the ocean, the water already beginning to feel the influence of the rising wind, and heaving up and down in long swells.

The clouds began to gather over the face of the moon, and partially to obscure its light.

Blakely's boat had come so near that the young man felt satisfied the unknown was within range of his revolver.

"Now hit her up, lads!" he said, drawing his revolver; "if we can hold our own for ten minutes more I may be able to either shoot or frighten him into submission."

"Ten minutes, yer honor, is 'bout all you've got," the old salt remarked. "For in that 'ere time he'll be round the Hook, and then with this hyar wind he'll fly from us like a bird."

The crew, excited by the chase, redoubled their efforts, the boat traveled through the water at a rapid pace. Blakely rose in the stern, deliberately cocked his revolver, and leveled it at the fugitive.

"Come about, or I'll put a ball through you!" he cried.

"Ha! ha! ha!"

Over the waves came the demoniac laugh of the stranger.

"For the last time, I demand that you surrender, or your blood will be upon your own head!"

"Fire, weak mortal fool! I defy alike fire, lead, or steel!" the other replied.

Coming to the conclusion that it was useless to waste words upon a man who was either rash to desperation, or else so nearly a lunatic that he did not comprehend the risk he was running, Blakely opened fire; but it was difficult to aim accurately in such a sea, and two shots went wide of the mark.

Again the fiend-like laugh of the unknown rung out shrilly on the air.

"By Jove! I will hit him this time!" Blakely cried, but even as he spoke the other craft ran round the point, and getting the full benefit of the wind, which suddenly strengthened just at that moment, flew over the surface of the waves like a sea- bird.

"The jig is up!" cried the old salt, in disgust.

Then up rose the unknown in the stern of his boat, and extending his arms in a peculiar fashion, laughed in demon-like glee.

The boat's crew lay on their oars, and every head was turned to watch the man. Many of them had sailed in southern seas, heard strange tales, and seen strange sights.

"Shiver my timbers! if it ain't the vampire!" old Tom Egan exclaimed.

CHAPTER VI.

"THE vampire!" exclaimed Blakely, echoing the words of the bo'swain.

"Ay, ay, yer honor, sure as you're born!" answered the old sailor. "No wonder the storm is up. What do you s'pose that 'ere critter keers for anything of that kind? Why, that's jest nuts to him! The harder it blows the better he likes it. Didn't he say that he wasn't afeard of anything mortal? Heaven help the poor gal, say I, for she's probably a gorner long afore now. No use chasin' the thing, for if we got up to it the odds are big that it would vanish in a clap of thunder."

And then, just as if the elements were listening to the sailor's words, a vivid flash of lightning came out of the clouds, followed by a low, rumbling peal of thunder.

More than one of the men in the boat started, for it seemed reasonable to the most of them that there might be some truth in the bo'swain's words.

The wind increased, the clouds thickened, so that for a few moments the light of the moon was obscured, and when its rays again struggled forth, the boat of the fugitives had gained such headway that it was clearly impossible it could be overtaken.

Reluctantly, Blakely gave orders to discontinue the chase, and, putting his boat about, headed for the ship.

The wind grew still stronger and the waves rolled high, tossing their white caps up toward the sky, which was covered with dark and angry-looking clouds.

Blakely cast an anxious glance behind; the little craft had now disappeared in the distance, swallowed up by the darkness.

"Well, whatever the fellow is, he'll have a rough time of it this night in that egg-shell of a boat off this dangerous shore, or else I'm no prophet."

"Lord love yer honor," cried old Tom, "the weather ain't any more to sich a critter as that than to the Flying Dutchman wo't used to beat about Cape Horn."

"I heered tell on a vampire once down in the Isle of Java," observed another old seaman. "It was nigh onto twenty years ago, and this hyar thing used for to light onto a sleeping man, w'ot was foolish enough fur to camp out in the woods, fan him with his wings so as fur to keep him from waking and suck his blood at the same time. I never see'd any of the things, tho' heered plenty of yarns 'bout them, but I allers reckoned it war a kind of a bird."

"Thar's whar you are out o' your reckoning, messmate!" the bo'swain exclaimed. "'Tain't a bird, or anything else w'ot's right an' nat'ral, but a sort of a devil w'ot comes in the shape of a big bird; it's got the figger of a man, but the wings of a bird, a kinder hitched onto a man's arm, and the only thing it can live on is human blood. Leastways, that's how the yarn was spun to me, and I reckon that it's nigh onto thirty years ago when I sailed in them southern seas."

"Well, all I know 'bout it is w'ot I heered. and I must say, bo'swain, I don't take much stock in the devil business, seeing as how I never yet run across any of the critters in the four quarters of this hyar globe that I've sailed in, man or boy, fur forty years," responded the other stoutly.

"Sho! 'tain't much use to argufy 'bout the matter, but I'm willing to leave it to Blakely," observed the bo'swain, evidently annoyed that this yarn should be doubted. "If the vampire ain't a devil, then I'm a land-lubber and don't know the taste of salt water."

Blakely was placed in a difficult position, for he saw that the sailor believed in the vampire story as firmly as he did in his own existence, and he hated to wound the old man's feelings by stating that modern opinion had rejected the vampire story as being entirely unworthy of belief, so he dodged the question.

"Well, Tom, it is one of those things that a man must form his own opinion about," he remarked. "That there is a big bird down in the lands of the tropics, which is accused of being a blood-sucker, and attacking sleeping men, is pretty generally believed, although some learned men dispute its existence, or at least deny that it attacks men, and that creature is called the vampire; and then, a good many years ago, almost everybody believed that there was a sort of a creature, not exactly human, yet wearing the human shape, a human in fact who, ought to be in the grave, but who managed to lead a sort of false life, by robbing his victims of theirs. For instance, suppose there was a girl twenty years-old, and whose natural term of life would be forty, that is if the vampire did not cut it short; by killing her and drinking her blood the vampire added the twenty years of her life to his own, and so he really became like the Wandering Jew, a being who would never die, provided he could always procure victims."

"That's it, yer honor; that's the yarn, just as I heered it spun a good thirty years ago!" the bo'swain exclaimed.

"Yes, yer honor; but I reckon that people nowadays don't take much stock in that hyar yarn, do they?" said the other seaman.

"Well, take the world at large, I suppose there isn't many who believe that such a thing exists now, or ever did exist, although in the old time a man would have been a laughing-stock for everybody if he had presumed to doubt the truth of the story."

"You see, Tom, you't have to back water on yer vampire yarn!" exclaimed the other old salt, triumphantly.

"Avast there, messmate, I ain't that kind of a marling-spike!" Tom replied. "W'ot does it matter w'ot folks say? Don't all the land-lubbers grin at the idea of the sea-sarpint, and whar's the able-bodied seaman wo't ain't seen the thing a dozen times?"

This was a knock-down lick, and the rest nodded their heads in approval.

"And don't they hoo, hoo, at mermaids? but we old sailors know that thar is sich things, if you'll take the trouble to go where they are. And this very night hain't we seen the vampire? Wasn't it a man with the wings of a bird? Kin any of you say that it wasn't? And do you s'pose any man with two grains of sense in his head would dare to run down the Jersey coast in such a night as this, in a boat like that? Why, if he don't go to Davy Jones' locker afore two hours are over it is because thar ain't anything human 'bout him or his craft."

"That's so, that's so," murmured the rest, and the other perceiving that the majority sided with the bo'swain gave up the discussion.

Of course Blakely was above yielding to such superstition; he knew well enough that the abductor was a man, and the only explanation he could give in regard to his singular conduct was that he was a little cracked in the upper story, for surely no man in his senses would thus rush to almost certain death.

By the time that the boat reached the steamer a regular gale was blowing.

Blakely made his report and the captain shook his head.

"It is a sad affair, Mr. Blakely, a mysterious one, too, for it's certain that no such boat as the one you describe can live off the Jersey coast on such a night as this, so it is almost impossible for the girl and her abductor to escape a watery grave."

All night long the storm continued, and it did not cease until after daybreak.

The steamer came up to her berth in the city, and as she was being slowly towed in to the wharf, Morgan and Lee encountered each other in the crowd which had congregated to wait the disembarkation of the passengers.

"I was at your house this morning!" Morgan exclaimed, "but they told me you had gone out. I thought it probable that you were busy about this affair and so I came down here."

"Oh, yes; I am not the man to waste precious moments or allow golden opportunities to escape me."

"Hello, there's Straub now," Morgan remarked, catching sight of the old lawyer in the crowd. "He has come in person to receive the girl. Suppose he sees us?"

"Well, what of it? Isn't it as likely for us to have friends on board the steamer as anybody else?" Lee replied. "He must be gifted with uncommon acuteness to suspect that our presence here can have aught to do with him, or with the girl."

"What is the programme? I presume you are proceeding on some definitely-arranged plan of operations."

"Oh, yes; I have mapped out the whole affair in my mind, and I have only come down here out of pure curiosity to see how the young lady looks."

"What is the game?"

"I have employed a couple of private detectives, and put them on Straub's track, so that he can't move without my knowledge. I want to ascertain where he puts the girl, find out what kind of a creature she is, and then I'll be able to decide in regard to the best mode of preventing her from interfering with our plans. We can't very well make headway against an enemy until we find out all about the opposing force. Then, too, I have bribed the lawyer's confidential clerk; he's a rascal, on a small salary, and jumped at the chance to make a hundred — there he is now; that sleek, oily-looking fellow at Straub's side — so I shall know all that he knows."

The steamer was at last made fast, and the old lawyer, accompanied by his clerk, hurried on board, only to be told the tale of the girl's mysterious disappearance.

An hour later the information, in all its details, was in Lee's possession.

"By Jove!" he exclaimed to Lee, discussing the matter, "we have put ourselves to a good deal of trouble for nothing, and I am a hundred out."

"It's mighty strange though, isn't it?"

"Yes; the chapter of accidents stood our friend. She may turn up again, though, and we must keep on the watch."

CHAPTER VII.

Of all the detectives in New York, none stood higher in the estimation of the superintendent of police than Sam Brace, and good reason had the chief for his confidence. In a dozen difficult cases Brace had proved himself the right man in the right place, and the dangerous classes, too, of great Gotham shared in the belief of the police superintendent that Brace was the most capable of all the city detectives, and many a bold ruffian had given leg bail, and fled from New York in hot haste when he heard that the celebrated detective was on his track.

Proteus-like, the police blood-hound was capable of assuming disguises so complete that his nearest and dearest friend would never suspect his identity, and, being a man of such rare ability, it was but natural that the hunting down of the mysterious assassin should be intrusted to him.

The detective puzzled over the matter for some time. He was of the superintendent's opinion that the murders were committed by a single assassin, although it was possible he might have assistance. He believed, too, that the doer of the deed rather gloried in the act and prided himself upon being able to baffle the skill of the police; but how to strike the trail of the mysterious murderer, unless found by accident, was a puzzle; finally, though, the detective hit upon a plan.

The victims were all elderly men and all strangers to New York. Now Brace, although not old, yet was not young, and being portly and massive in form, had little difficulty in transforming himself into a fine specimen of the traveling Briton, side-whiskers, eye-glasses, accent and all. He even went to the trouble to go clear to Albany, and assume his disguises there, then came down the river by boat, accompanied by a well-known sole leather trunk, sticking to which were labels, apparently testifying that it had been half over the world.

Upon arriving in the city the detective had caused himself to be driven with considerable display to the leading up-town hotels, where he registered as Major Roger Sharp, London, England.

The detective's scheme was an extremely simple one. He intended, in the guise of an elderly stranger, with plenty of money, to flaunt in all the public places of the city, thinking, thereby, to attract the attention of the mysterious assassin, who, regarding him an easy prey, would be lured to the attack, and so discover himself.

It was a bold game to play, for there was a slight possibility that the unknown murderer had his plans so well arranged that the man caught within the toils was not allowed a single chance of escaping with life from the snare.

The detective, however, was willing to run the risk of this, for he agreed that there was a deal of difference between himself, armed to the teeth, fully prepared for the encounter, and the unfortunate victims who, probably, had not the slightest suspicion that danger threatened until they were in a position to receive the fatal blow and all means of escape cut off.

Brace had arranged with the superintendent to have men posted at certain points, day and night, so that he could communicate with headquarters if the necessity arose, but so exceedingly careful was the detective in the carrying out of his scheme, that neither the men, his comrades, nor even the superintendent himself, had the slightest inkling in regard to his disguise.

A week passed away, and though the disguised detective had been approached by a half dozen rascals, all intent upon making him a victim, yet when he had followed each and every one up, which he did with the utmost patience, they all turned out to be petty, common scoundrels, not worth wasting time upon.

"By Jove!" muttered the detective, as he pursued his promenade along Broadway and up Fifth Avenue, one pleasant afternoon, "is it possible that the fellow has given up the business, retired rich, or in some mysterious way discovered that I am on his track?"

And just as Brace had come to the conclusion that he was wasting time and might as well give the matter up as a bad job, a lady passing glanced at him in a peculiar way.

Now, the detective, although a bachelor, was noted on the force for being quite a lady's man, and from the glance that he received from the fair unknown he came to the conclusion that she would not be displeased to make his acquaintance.

Brace was a fine-looking man, and even though his disguise made him appear ten or fifteen years older than he really was, yet it did not destroy his personal appearance.

The lady was young and good-looking, dark-eyed, and dark-haired; Brace could make this out, although she wore a light, fleecy veil that in a measure concealed her features. She was dressed in the most exquisite taste, wore rich jewelry, not gaudy, but just enough for adornment, and it was plain that she was a lady by birth, breeding, and station.

"By George!" muttered the detective, using his favorite exclamation, as he turned and followed in the wake of the woman, "it would be odd if in this disguise I should succeed in fascinating some Murray Hill dame. If I should happen to pick up a rich wife now, wouldn't it be a stroke of luck? She looks a little like a foreigner, and if she is perhaps it will not be difficult to make her acquaintance, for those ladies raised abroad are not so deuced particular, after they have reached a certain age, as our American girls."

Upon reaching Broadway the lady sauntered along, looking in the shop windows, and every now and then casting a shy glance behind her in such a manner that the detective felt perfectly sure she was aware he was following her, and was not displeased at him for doing so.

When she reached Union Square the detective was only a few steps behind her, and she took advantage of the fact that the sidewalk was for the moment deserted to "accidentally" drop her handkerchief.

Brace understood that this was done for his especial benefit, and he was quick to improve the opportunity.

Picking up the handkerchief he hastened forward and accosted the lady.

"I beg your pardon, miss, you have dropped your handkerchief," and he tendered it to her with his most gallant bow.

With an air of charming confusion the lady received it, and then discovered that one of the bangles attached to her bracelet was missing.

"I wouldn't have lost it for the world," she declared, speaking with a slight foreign accent. "It must have become detached since I came out, for I am sure it was on the bracelet when I started. I came down the avenue to Broadway."

"Strange coincidence! that is exactly the way I came. If you will permit me, I will accompany you on your return and assist you to look for the trinket."

The lady appeared confused, cast down her eyes, half blushes, and murmured something about "being sorry to trouble a stranger," but Brace gallantly protested that it wasn't the least bit of trouble, produced his card-case — he had taken the precaution to provide himself with a "pasteboard," got up in stunning style — and she, evidently impressed with the idea that her companion was a man of consequence, accepted his escort without further words.

And as they walked up the street it was the most natural thing in the world for them to fall into conversation. Brace explained who he was — "gave her the English art," as he would have said in the slang of his trade, and she told her story.

As he had guessed, she was of foreign birth. French, but she had lived so long in this country that it seemed like her native land. She was called Hortense Thibault, was a widow, having lost her husband, who was in the tobacco trade, some two years before. She had had considerable trouble in settling up her husband's estate, owing to the fact that his business connections were mainly with foreign parties, but now she had come to the end of her trouble, and was prepared to enjoy life, although she was such a stranger in New York, having, during her husband's lifetime, resided principally in the South, that she had hardly an acquaintance in the city.

Brace was in the seventh heaven of delight; evidently he had stumbled upon an unexpected piece of good fortune. The detective was too shrewd a man not to closely scrutinize the lady while she was relating her story, for the thought had naturally come to him that it might possibly be a "plant;" the lady might be a confidence operator, seeking to entrap him, but by the time she had ended her recital, he was satisfied not only that the story was correct, but that after the fashion common to some women she had taken a most prodigious fancy to him at first sight.

Here was a windfall with a vengeance; a young and pretty widow, with a fortune too, apparently a pretty big one, from the carelessness with which she spoke about money, and there didn't seem to be the least obstacle in the way of winning the lady if he chose to play his game correctly.

In charming confusion she invited him to go with her to her home, and seemed delighted when he accepted.

Her house was in one of the up-town cross streets, a handsome though small brown-stone front, with a stable in the rear.

Brace was ushered into the parlor, and with her own hands the fair widow brought cakes and wine, and challenged him to pledge her health in the ruddy vintage of the grape.

The glasses clinked and they drank, but no sooner had the detective swallowed the draught than his senses began to desert him.

The room swam around his giddy head.

Too late he knew the truth.

He was drugged and in the toils.

CHAPTER VIII.

NINE days had passed since Brace had taken up his quest, and, as no word had come from him in all that time, the superintendent began to wonder what on earth had become of him.

So perfect had been the detective's disguise that, although he had passed by the men appointed to act in concert with him a dozen times, and they were as well acquainted with him as though they were all his own brothers, yet not a single man recognized him.

The chief became alarmed as time passed on and he neither saw nor heard from the detective. A fear took possession of his mind that some mischance had befallen him, and he caused a secret alarm to be sent out, but nothing came of it; no one had seen or heard of the detective since he departed on his mission.

It was just possible, of course, that Brace had hit upon some clew which, to follow up, had caused him to go out of town, but the superintendent was not satisfied with this theory, for he felt sure Brace would never have left town without notifying him.

Both the governor and the mayor, having been informed that the detective had undertaken the task of discovering the secret assassin, and knowing the ability of the man, had great hopes that he would succeed in solving the bloody mystery, and they called upon the superintendent frequently, anxious for intelligence, hoping that the detective had hit the trail, and that there was a probability of the discovery of the assassin.

On the ninth day after the blood-hound of the law had set forth upon the search, the two officials were closeted with the police chief, and they plainly expressed their diappointment when the superintendent reported that he had not the slightest bit of news to offer.

"Well, what do you think about it?" the governor asked. "What is your opinion in regard to the matter? Isn't it strange that you haven't received any word whatever from Brace?"

"Yes it is," the chief admitted, "and I must say I regard it as a bad sign, although the old adage says that no news is good news, but I can't make up my mind that it is so in this case; it is just possible that Brace has got on the track of the rascal, and the fellow finding it out has fled -"

"Yes it is possible; but not probable."

Just at that moment the chief's secretary came in with a letter which had been left by the carrier. A peculiar-looking letter, addressed to the Superintendent of the New York Police, but instead of the superscription upon the envelope being written, it was formed of printed letters, of different sizes, evidently cut out from a newspaper, and pasted upon the envelope.

The chief laughed as he showed the letter to his visitors.

"This ought to be something important," he observed, "for the person that sent it is so afraid his handwriting will be recognized, that he has employed this device to prevent discovery. It is an old trick, and yet as a general rule such letters seldom amount to anything."

The superintendent opened the envelope carefully with his pen-knife, drew out the sheet of foolscap paper within, and when that was unfolded, the communication was found to be composed of the same printed characters as formed the address.

"By Heaven! gentlemen, this refers to the very subject we were talking about!" the chief exclaimed, as he glanced at the message. "Listen!

"'Have you missed your detective, Brace? Do you want to know where he is? Be at the lower end of the City Hall Park tonight at twelve, and a man will be there to give you a pointer. Keep it dark.'

"No signature, gentlemen, as you will observe, and each word is a printed one, cut from a newspaper, evidently, and pasted on the letter; this fellow was determined that we should not have a clew as to who he was by his handwriting."

"What do you think about it — what does it mean?" the governor asked.

"As far as I can make out, it signifies that Brace, instead of trapping the scoundrels, has fallen into a snare himself. This seems to say that there is a gang at the bottom of the business. I don't generally take much stock in letters of this kind, but I believe there is something in this. The fellow that sent it knows evidently that Brace is absent on important detective business, and that I am bothered by not hearing from him. Of course there are leaks in all offices, but I think I have contrived to keep this matter pretty quiet; so it would seem as if this communication really came from some one who knows what has become of Brace and is disposed to make use of his knowledge."

"But if the writer is one of the band, why should he betray the secret?"

"Going to peach on his accomplices — turn state's evidence, you know;" replied the superintendent.

"These rascals are seldom true to each other if they can make a stake by turning informer. If it wasn't for these sneaks we shouldn't make much headway, sometimes."

"You are satisfied that there isn't any humbug about it?" the governor asked, rather suspicious.

"What object would any one have in sending such a letter unless they meant business?"

"None at all," remarked the mayor, "unless some fool was doing it for a joke."

"Yes, there are plenty of such idiots in the world, but a practical joker would not be apt to have any knowledge of this business," the superintendent replied. "No, gentlemen, I think you will find that it will turn out to be about as I say. Brace got on the track of the scoundrels, just as I felt certain he would; ventured into their den, single-handed, expecting only to collar one man, for he believed with me that there wasn't but a single hand in the business; the odds were too great and they 'downed' him, and that is the reason why I haven't heard anything from him. Now one of the gang has 'taken a tumble' to himself and thinks he can make a stake by giving the thing away."

The others nodded; the theory seemed reasonable.

"So, gentlemen, at twelve to-night I will be at the appointed spot."

"I'll go with you, if my presence will not interfere with the business in hand!" exclaimed the mayor.

"Not at all!"

"And I will make one of the party," the governor added.

"I shall be glad of your company, gentlemen, for I think that the author of this communication means business. I will have a squad of men near at hand ready for action, if any immediate work is required. I am sorry for Brace; it will be a dreadful blow to him if the fellows have captured his precious person, and it takes a squad to snake him out of their hands. He'll be disgusted, for, so far in his professional career, he has been very successful, and has worked up some cases that would do credit to any detective in the world, bar none."

"At twelve, then," said the governor, as he and the mayor arose.

"Yes, but we want to start about a quarter before. Suppose I met you at the Fifth Avenue Hotel? I will have a coach, and it will give us ample time to reach the spot, if we start from the hotel at a quarter before twelve."

To this the others agreed and then deputed.

The superintendent arranged to have a squad of half a dozen of his best men in the neighborhood of the park at twelve exactly, and managed the matter so that they could reach the locality without any one suspecting their presence in the vicinity.

"The bird is probably a wary customer, and I must be careful not to frighten him away before he sings his little song," the police officer observed.

Not the slightest thought that there might be personal danger in the quest ever entered the brain of the superintendent. He knew the rogues of New York too well; no five or ten of them would have dared to attack the superintendent in the open street no matter what the hour.

Promptly that night, at a quarter to twelve, the two officials were at the Fifth Avenue Hotel, and equally as promptly the superintendent made his appearance in a coach.

The mayor and the governor got in, and away they went.

Right to the minute, just as the bells tolled the midnight hour, the three men alighted from the back at the Broadway side of the park, near the City Hall.

"Remain here, gentlemen, please." said the police official, "while I go forward and see what the party is made of; it will not do for all of us to go, for if the rascal saw three men, he would be apt to suspect that there was a trap, and refrain from putting in an appearance. When a fish of this sort is hooked, he has to be played very carefully, or you'll never land him."

The others saw the wisdom of this course, and so they remained by the back while the superintendent walked to the end of the park.

City Hall Park formerly ran to a point at the lower end, but the General Post Office has been built upon that particular spot, and a broad street, for the convenience of the mail teams, so that they can reach the rear doors of the building, separates the post-office from the park.

At the edge of the street the chief halted and looked around him. He reached the spot just as the bell gave the final stroke of the hour.

No one was in sight; ten, fifteen minutes the official waited, but no one came; then the figure of a man, half-reclining in an angle of the building opposite, attracted his attention.

"I wonder if that is the party, and he has fallen asleep."

The chief crossed the street and laid his hand upon the man's shoulder.

It was the detective, Brace, cold in death!

CHAPTER IX.

Juan Anchona was one of the representative men of New York. He had entered the great metropolis years ago, when the city was a small town, indeed, compared to what it now is; a poor boy, yet with an indomitable will, he had worked his way up until the banking house of Anchona was as well known, and its influence as great, as that of any other establishment in this same line of business in the country.

Anchona was one of the so-called successful men; everything he touched seemed to turn into gold; and it was a joke in the commercial world, when any one of note became interested in a losing speculation, for the "Street" to say: "Get Anchona to take hold of it, and then you will see the money come tumbling in."

In person the banker was a tall, portly man, well preserved for his years, being over seventy, with a massive face, betraying his resolute nature in every line, fringed with iron-gray hair, and illuminated by a pair of keen gray eyes, that showed little trace of the ravages of time.

Like most men who have fought the world successfully, and acquired a commanding position and colossal wealth, Anchona had an imperious way and was impatient of contradiction. He had been so long accustomed to having all his schemes progress to a successful end that the miscarriage of his plans in regard to the girl annoyed him greatly, and even Straub, who was used to his moods, having been his confidential adviser and attended to all his important and private business for years, was amazed at the irritation which he displayed about the matter.

When the lawyer had returned from the steamer and related the story of the disappearance of the girl, the old gentleman had flown into the most violent passion.

"It is a plot — a conspiracy to extort money from me!" he declared, jumping to his feet and pacing up and down the confines of his library with the restlessness of a caged lion.

"A conspiracy to extort money!" cried the old lawyer, utterly unable to comprehend what his client was driving at.

"Yes, yes. I understand it all: but the rascals will find that the game will not work. They have the girl — they can keep her for all that I shall do, and much good may they get out of her! But if they think to use her as a weapon against me, they never made a greater mistake in all their lives!"

"But Mr. Anchona, I do not understand -"

"Of course not! of course not!" the other cried, impatiently. "You cannot be expected to understand a matter of which you know absolutely nothing. I tell you it is a plot. I can see it at a glance: and I have been afraid of something of the kind all the time. I suspected that there might be certain parties base enough to follow the girl from England and try and use her as a weapon against me the moment she got on this side of the water. They discovered I had sent for her, and they laid their plans accordingly."

"Mr. Anchona, I trust you will excuse me for being obliged to differ with you," the lawyer said. He was a stately, white-haired gentleman of the old school, very polite and very precise.

"Well, how do you differ?"

"Your statement that some one in England discovered that you had sent for the girl cannot possibly be correct, for you did not appear in the matter at all; in fact, so cautious was I in arranging the details of the affair, so that your agency should not be suspected, that I myself did not appear in the transaction, but the business was done in the name of one of the clerks in my office; so, Mr. Anchona, you may rest assured, as far as the affair itself is concerned, no one in England could possibly have suspected that you had anything to do with it. In fact, I do not see how any one, either here or elsewhere, could have known anything of it, for I was careful not to speak about the matter to a soul, and as it was known only to us, I do not comprehend how it could have leaked out."

By this time Anchona had recovered in a measure from the violent passion into which he had been thrown, and upon reflecting upon the matter, he was obliged to admit the truth of the lawyer's remarks.

"Besides, the young man on board of the steamer, from whom I received the particulars of the strange affair, informed me that there wasn't any doubt in his mind that the man who carried off the girl got on board the steamer by means of a small boat when she came to anchor off quarantine."

"But the motive for the crime?" Anchona questioned. "There must have been some powerful motive, for a man wouldn't put himself in jeopardy by so willfully defying the law without a good and sufficient reason."

"That is very true, and that is what occurred to me the moment I heard the particulars and questioned the young man in regard to it. He was a sensible, intelligent fellow, and came to the point at once, with all a sailor's frankness. He thought the man was crazy."

"Crazy!" exclaimed the banker.

"Yes; he had a talk with the fellow on the deck, just before the abduction occurred; he noticed something peculiar about the man, and got the idea that he was not a passenger, and naturally was puzzled to account for his presence on the ship. He asked his name, then went to examine the passenger lists, and when he returned the man had rendered the girl insensible in some way, and in a small boat was making off. Chase was at once given, but a storm came up, and the abductor, with his victim, escaped by running out to sea."

"It is the strangest affair that I ever knew of in all my experience," the banker remarked, reflectively. "Of course, my dear Straub, I have more than a stranger's interest in this girl, and there are weighty reasons for that interest; one of these days you shall know all, but for the present I will retain the secret. I have sedulously kept myself in the background in the matter, for fear there might be parties in England, who, if they learned I was interesting myself in the girl, would strive to see her as a tool to wring money from me, knowing I was a man of means. Mind, I am not sure that any such parties exist; I only took precautions in case they did; but as to any one on this side of the water troubling their heads about the girl, it looks altogether impossible; for while it was probable that there might be persons in England who knew something about her and her family, it is certain there wasn't any one in America besides myself who did. My unfortunate brother, who fell by the hand of this secret assassin, had some slight knowledge, but that I imparted to him, and now he is dead. I alone know aught of her."

"It is certainly a mysterious affair, and the supposition of the young man, Mr. Blakely, who is third officer of the City of Chester, that the deed was perpetrated by a lunatic, seems to be the only reasonable explanation."

"By the bye, how would it do for me to see this gentleman?" asked Anehona, abruptly. "Possibly he might be able to suggest something. I do not feel disposed to leave the matter in this unsatisfactory state. After bringing the girl clear from England, I object to having her taken out of my hands in this unceremonious manner."

"It would be an excellent idea."

"Suppose you see him and bring him up as soon as convenient."

"Very well; my time is my own to-day, and I'll hunt him up."

The lawyer departed, and acted so promptly in the matter, and was so favored by circumstances, that within two hours be returned accompanied by Mr. Blakely.

The young man was introduced to the banker by the lawyer, and at the first glance Anchona, who prided himself upon his judgment in reading character, took a fancy to the gentleman, and so, without hesitation, he confided to him the deep interest which he took in the abducted girl.

"Mr. Straub informs me," he said in conclusion, "that it is your belief that the man who committed this most atrocious crime was not exactly right in his head."

"Yes, sir, that was the opinion I formed, although from the conversation I had with him on the steamer's deck, just before the act was committed, I should not have suspected that there was anything the matter with him, but when I chased him in the boat, while the storm was rising, and I threatened him with my revolver, then he most certainly acted like a man who was a little cracked in the upper story."

"Could you imagine any motive that the man could possibly have for the outrageous act?"

"None at all; I am satisfied that he was a stranger to the girl, and gained access to the deck of the steamer by means of the same small boat in which he escaped, and there not being the slightest reason for the deed, as far as I can see, is why I am impressed with the belief that it was due to the witless freak of a lunatic."

"It looks like it! Upon my soul it does!" Anchona exclaimed.

The old lawyer agreed with this.

"But now the point is — what has become of the girl?" the banker asked.

Blakely shook his head.

"I am afraid, sir, that the ruffian, whether sane or a lunatic, hurried both himself and the girl to certain death. He was in a small boat, the storm was high, and the coast dangerous."

"But there is a chance that they might have escaped?"

"Yes, sir, a chance."

"Are you at liberty to accept a commission to look into the matter? — never mind the expense, I will stand that, no matter what it costs."

Blakely accepted the offer gladly, for he was deeply interested, and half an hour later he was on his way to the Jersey coast.

CHAPTER X.

AND what was the fate of the boat which, like a phantom craft, fled tossing on the raging billows into the darkness of the night?

The sea was raging mountains high, and the wind kept steadily increasing in strength. The boat, running straight before the gale, raced onward at almost incredible speed.

The craft was almost half a mile from the land, and every now and then, when the lightning's flash illuminated the darkness of the night, the low outline of the Jersey coast could be distinctly observed.

"Now, then, follow me if you dare!" the unknown had shouted in wild glee, as he ran past the low, sandy point of the Hook into the open sea, and with a turn of the wrist, pointed the prow of the boat to the southward, thus getting the full benefit of the wind.

As he had anticipated, the other boat gave up the chase, and as he cast a glance backward and beheld them pull around, he laughed in a wild, fierce glee.

"Aha, you cowards! you don't dare to follow me!" he cried, "and you are wise not to attempt it, for I would lead you to certain death! Oh, isn't this glorious? This is life — this is worth living for! How the balmy breeze fans my fevered cheek and cools my heated brain!" And then again the man laughed in wild delight, and if Blakely could have heard him he would have been certain that his guess had been right when he came to the conclusion that the man was a lunatic.

When the stranger again looked behind him the pursuing boat had disappeared.

"The blind fools to imagine that they could overtake me, and all the advantages on my side!" he exclaimed, scornfully.

"But have they given up the chase?" he cried abruptly, after quite a long silence. He was keeping the boat right straight before the wind and racing along at a speed of fully ten knots an hour.

"No, no, it is not likely," he muttered, after cogitating over the matter for a while. "That young puppy has taken a fancy to the girl. I saw that in his face; and that is the reason why he pursued me so hotly. He is a sailor and knows that he might as well chase a will-o'-the-wisp as follow me over the open sea, but he is of a bull-dog breed and will not give up the pursuit while a chance remains. He cannot follow me in the teeth of this gale, but he can wait in the calmer water inside of Sandy Hook to intercept me when I return. Yes, yes! that will be his plan undoubtedly; but what chance is there for its success on such a night as this, with the storm raging, the sky black with angry clouds, and all so dark that, excepting when lightning flashes, not an object can be distinguished a hundred feet distant? A single boat could hardly succeed in patroling the entrance on a clear night, let alone in the face of such a storm as this. My game is simple enough; I will go about and make for the Long Island shore and slip up into the bay under the lee of the land."

It was a noticeable fact that now the man was communing with himself, there was not a particle of foreign accent perceptible in his voice, which plainly showed that the accent was not natural but assumed.

The girl, the victim of the outrage, had been placed in the bow of the boat, and the man had not paid the least attention to her, until now, when a movement on her part showed him that the influence of the drug, which had stupefied her, was passing away.

Slowly the use of her senses came back, and at last she sat up and stared around. She was still so confused that she did not realize what had occurred; she was like one wandering in the mazes of a horrid dream.

But as she looked upon the waste of waters, shut in by the inky darkness of the night, and then caught sight of the striking features of the stranger, crouching in the stern, all at once she realized what had taken place, but when she did, she was even more bewildered, if such a thing could be, than before.

She understood that she was the victim of a foul outrage — she had been abducted from the deck of the steamer by this man, whose evil eyes seemed to glare at her with a demoniac power, but why had this been done? what motive was there for so foul a deed? She had not been injured — had escaped bodily harm, excepting that she felt weak and faint from the effects of the drug which she had been forced to inhale.

The few trinkets she wore had not cost five dollars, and surely no one would be silly enough to imagine she had money concealed about her person; what then could any one gain by perpetrating so great a crime?

"You have recovered your senses, I perceive," the man observed.

"What does this mean?" she exclaimed.

"I do not understand," and he assumed an ignorant air.

"You know well enough! Why have you committed this gross outrage? What did I ever do to you that you should assault me in so cruel a manner?"

"Oh, you are still in a delirium, I see," he observed. "My dear girl, you must try and call back your wandering senses. No one has harmed you. You have been carried off for a little pleasure excursion, that is all."

"You will pay dearly for this when the law seizes you in its iron grip," exclaimed the exasperated girl.

"When the law seizes me!" and then the man laughed in such a fiendish way that it fairly made the blood of the hapless maiden run cold, "And how soon do you suppose that interesting event will take place?"

"The moment I have reached the shore, for then I will instantly denounce you."

"Ha, ha, ha!" and again the abductor laughed loud and long. "Do you really suppose that you are ever going to reach the shore?" and the man infused into the question such a terrible meaning that Helena, despite her undoubted courage, could not help shuddering.

"Just consider the situation!" he continued. "Here you are, in a frail boat, the wind blowing a gale, increasing in force as the night advances, off one of the most dangerous shores in the country. Were it not for the howling of the wind we could hear the roar of the surf on the sand, the merciless breakers, that seldom part with a victim that they get within their clutches while life remains, and then the mangled, mutilated corpse is tossed, as if in contempt, high upon the beach."

"I am not afraid of the waves — I am not afraid of the wind; the hand of an all-powerful Ruler is in both," she cries.

"But you do fear me!" he answered, abruptly.

"Yes, it is true; for I believe you are a creature of the lost soul who reigns in the realms of darkness." And so she did; if it had been possible for a girl as well educated and intelligent as Helena to believe in the old time traditions that for certain purposes, fiends were sometimes permitted to assume the mortal shape, then she would have been most surely convinced that the helmsman who faced her with such a sinister expression upon his saturnine features was no man of flesh and blood. But as it was she knew enough of the world to understand that there are some mortals who seem born under an evil star, being as malignant in their natures as the followers of the fallen angel.

"And you are right, too, dear, for never in all your life were you menaced by a more terrible danger than that which threatens you. Why do you suppose I have taken the trouble to carry you off?"

"I cannot understand — it is a mystery to me."

"Did you ever see me before?"

"Never."

"You are sure, then, that I am not an old foe with an ancient grudge against you?"

"Yes, because I have no foes," she replied, in a simple, earnest way. "I have never wronged any one, and I am sure there isn't any reason why you, or any one else, should wish to injure me."

"Did the idea ever enter your head that there might be a man in this world possessed of so animal a nature that blood was congenial to him? a man of such unnatural instincts that he killed merely for the pleasure of killing."

The breath of the girl came quick and fast as she listened to those horrid words, and having her eyes fixed intently upon the man's face, her wits rendered unnaturally sharp by the peculiar position in which she was placed, she fancied she could detect a gleam in his eyes which denoted that his wits were disordered; and immediately she remembered that she had often read that when one was dealing with insane persons it is always best to humor them in their delusions, and so, resolving to act upon this idea, she took heart a little.

That her abductor was not in his right senses was a reasonable explanation for his outrageous conduct, for, otherwise, there was not the slightest excuse for what had taken place.

"Oh, yes, such a thing might to possible," she replied, with a great effort forcing herself to appear calm.

"You believe that?"

"Yes; I presume it is not improbable."

"How about the vampire?" he asked, abruptly.

"The vampire!" she echoed, not understanding him.

"Yes, the vampire; do you believe in vampires?"

"I don't know,"' the girl replied, bewildered.

"You know the story of the vampire," he continued, rapidly, his eyes swelling with unnatural fires. "The human who leads an artificial life — who lives on the blood he extracts from his victims — that he sucks from their very veins, drawing the red life-current directly from the heart!"

"Oh, merciful heavens!" moaned the girl, almost paralyzed with terror.

"It is not a fable; such things do exist as you will find to your cost before this night is over; the old life-current ebbs freely in the veins, and a new supply is needed — fresh, young blood. You should live thirty — forty years yet, but you will die to-night, and the years of your life will go to enrich an-other! Now we will return."

He essayed to put the boat about, but managed it so badly that it fell into the trough of a wave.

The mast snapped, the boat upset, and out into the raging sea went both captor and captive.

CHAPTER XI.

Horror-stricken, the police superintendent started back and gazed for a moment in speechless amazement upon the fearful sight.

It was the detective, Brace, beyond a doubt, and from the extremely natural manner in which the body had been propped up in the door way not one person out of a hundred would have suspected that the form was aught but that of a sleeping man.

"Dead, as I am a living sinner!" the police chief ejaculated, so overwhelmed by the unexpected discovery that he was for a few moments unable to do anything but stand and stare at the frightful sight.

"Oh, this is terrible!" he muttered. The superintendent, in the course of his busy professional life, had looked upon many dead bodies, but never upon one that had inspired him so with horror.

At last, with a great effort rousing himself front the shock, he hurried to where he had left the two officials, and they, perceiving by the expression upon his face that something out of the common had occurred, plied him with questions.

"Well, well, you have struck something, I see!" the governor exclaimed.

"Is Brace safe — the rascals haven't hurt him, I hope?" the mayor added.

"He is yonder, gentlemen, and you must prepare yourselves for an unpleasant sight," responded the chief in a sad voice, as he turned upon his heel to retrace his steps.

The others, although devoured by eager curiosity, refrained from further questions, for they guessed from the chief's words, simple though they were, that some terrible calamity had befallen the detective officer.

When the three came within the shadows of the post-office building the superintendent directed their attention to the body.

"Is he asleep?" asked the governor.

"Not under the influence of liquor, I hope?" quoth the mayor.

"He will never sleep or drink more, gentlemen; he is dead," answered the police official.

The others recoiled — an exclamation of horror came from their lips.

"He succeeded in his mission, as I felt sure he would; he found the assassin, but it was only to perish by his hand," said the chief, slowly and sadly.

"Oh, this is terrible!" cried the governor, really unnerved by the fearful discovery.

"Perfectly frightful, superintendent! this blood-thirsty villain must be hunted down and brought to justice, no matter what it costs!" the mayor exclaimed. "The whole power of the department must be brought to bear upon this case. Why, by this atrocious crime the villain actually shows that he laughs at the exertions of the police; the killing of this unfortunate man is nothing more than a bold defiance."

"Your honor, that is a conclusion that cannot be escaped, but before we proceed further in the matter, or counsel in regard to new measures, it will be as well to have a careful examination made of the body, for by so doing we may be able to gain some points."

The others admitted the wisdom of this course, so the police were summoned and the body removed.

Brace had indeed fallen by the hand of the mysterious assassin, for an examination revealed that he had perished from a stab wound piercing the heart, and on the neck, under the left ear, were the two mysterious marks which had also appeared on the bodies of the other victims.

The detective was dressed in his conspicuous Scotch tweed suit, in the vest pocket of which was a single card bearing the name which the detective had assumed. His wig and whiskers had been removed, though, and the card was the only article that was found upon his person. But it was quite enough to give the chief a clew to the part which the detective had been playing, particularly as the superintendent's attention one day at the Fifth Avenue Hotel had been attracted by the supposed stranger, and he had inquired who he was, never suspecting that the imposing-looking foreigner was his own favorite in disguise.

After the examination the three held a long private conversation.

The governor favored giving the matter the widest possible publicity — by offering a large reward for the apprehension of the assassin, thinking thereby to stimulate some private party to attempt the capture of the mysterious murderer, but the superintendent, after the fashion of the majority of men in his position, did not at all believe in the scheme.

"Better to keep it dark," he argued: "if we allow the newspapers to learn all the details of the affair, it will be blazoned forth to the world, and the perpetrator of the deed will be able to find out exactly how much we know, and so can take measures against discovery. Of course we can't keep Brace's death a secret, but we can let it go to the public that he was assaulted and killed by some unknown parties, that the police have a clew and are on the track of the murderer, but not breathe a word that we know that the secret assassin, who has so far baffled all the efforts of the police, was alto his slayer."

The mayor was rather inclined to side with the governor in his belief that all the details had better be given to the public, but finally both came to the conclusion that the adage, "Each man to his trade," was a wise one, and as there wasn't any doubt that the superintendent had much greater experience in rascal catching than they, it was probable the course he advocated was the wisest one to follow.

"We will leave the matter in your hands, then," the governor said, in conclusion. "but, Mr. Superintendent, this mysterious murder must be discovered: no man, or party of men, can be allowed to set the law at defiance in this audacious way."

"I will stake all the reputation that I have in police matters to hunt the villain down in time," the chief exclaimed, "but, governor, you must remember that I am only a man, and cannot be expected to perform impossible feats. It is a regular game that this fellow is playing, and, as it is evident he is exceedingly skillful, until he makes a false move it will be impossible for us to trip him; but the moment he does that — and he is sure to do it in the long run, for the pitcher that goes often to the well will be broken at last —

then we will have him on the hip, and he'll find himself in the Tombs before he knows what has happened."

This was the old "cheap" talk that police officials have indulged in ever since there have been thieves and thief-takers; but it satisfied the listeners, and they departed, full of confidence that in time the mysterious assassin, who had struck so many and such terrible blows, would be in the stern grasp of the law which he had so fearfully outraged.

To do the superintendent justice, he did set to work with uncommon vigor. He thought, and rightly, that the killing of the detective was a direct "slap" in the face for him, as he expressed it; his pride was wounded, and he determined to prove to the secret slayer that he had aroused no mean antagonist when he dared to defy the superintendent of the New York police.

Barely two hours' sleep did the chief have that night, for his brain was so busily engaged in revolving plans to entrap the unknown murderer that slumber wooed him in vain. It was not until he had totally worn himself out, alternately scheming and uttering imprecations upon the head of the unknown, that he fell asleep.

In the morning his first move was to send out a general alarm in regard to the "Englishman," Robert Sharp.

He had guessed the trick that Brace had set out to work. As the Englishman, he had hoped to induce the secret murderer to attack him. He had succeeded in his design, but instead of capturing the villain, had fallen a victim to his wiles. It was the old story of catching a Tartar — the trapper entrapped.

By the alarm one slight bit of information the chief gained.

The roundsman who "covered" that part of Broadway near Union Square, reported that three or four days before — he was uncertain as to the exact day — he had noticed a man, who resembled the description given of the Englishman, on the opposite side of the street — he was on the park sidewalk at the time — stoop and pick up a handkerchief which a lady dropped; then the two entered into conversation, and finally went up the street to-gether. The roundsman paid no particular attention to the little episode, for, as he expressed it, he thought it a clear case of "mashing," and wondered what it would cost the swell before he got out of the scrape.

"The woman! what was she like?" questioned the police chief, in almost breathless eagerness.

The roundsman was at fault; he admitted that he hadn't particularly noticed her. She was "kinder stylish," dressed in dark clothes, he "thought," but he wasn't sure.

"Would you be able to identify her if you met her again?" This was a critical question, and the roundsmat, after meditating about the matter for a few minutes, trying to freshen up his memory, was finally obliged to admit that he was pretty sure he would not be able so to do.

Here was a clew and yet not a clew. A woman had been with the disguised detective. He had gone with her, and that was the only trace of Brace that could be discovered, with the exception of the information furnished by the clerks of the hotel in regard to his procuring accommodations there.

Was the woman the secret assassin, or was she but a decoy used by the murderer to lure his victims into his net?

It did not seem possible that the murder could be the work of a woman's hand.

While the chief was pondering over the problem a visitor entered. The superintendent uttered a joyous cry. It was Carlton Brand, the keen detective.

CHAPTER XII.

"By heavens, Brand, you are the very man I wanted!" the superintendent exclaimed, rising and shaking hands with his visitor in the most cordial manner.

To those readers who have never made the acquaintance a few words of explanation are due.

Brand was one of the most remarkable men whose name was ever recorded in the police annals of New York.

A man possessed of wonderful physical power, undaunted courage, and a face so mobile that it was capable of the most astonishing changes, coupled with the instinct of a bloodhound, a more terrible man-catcher never got upon a rascal's track.

At first, Brand had been in the pay of the police, then had set up a private detective bureau of his own, but for some two years he had not been seen in New York; why he had disappeared, or where he had gone, no one knew.

And from this fact the chief, while looking for some man to put upon the track of the mysterious murderer, never thought of Brand, but the moment that gentleman made his appearance the idea instantly occurred to him, that of all the human sleuth-hounds in existence, Brand was the best who could be chosen to get to the heart of the strange and bloody mystery.

"Yes, yes; you are the very man I want," the chief repeated. "I've a job for you, if you are open to accept a commission: but I say, what have you been doing all this time? Where have you kept yourself?"

"I have been on a journey around the world."

"Ah! around the world for sport, eh?"

"No, on business. A confidential clerk absconded from New York, carrying off a large sum of money and some private papers which involved the honor of an old family. I was commissioned to hunt the man down, recover the money, if possible, although that was a secondary consideration, but at all hazards, and without regard to expense, to secure the papers."

"And the fellow led you a lively chase?"

"Yes; for nearly two years, but I finally ran him to earth in Brazil."

"No extradition treaty — that was ugly," observed the chief.

"There are more ways than one to kill a cat," Brand answered, in that calm and grave way, full of quiet dignity which was natural to him. "I had anticipated that it was possible, with the start he had, he might succeed in reaching some country, under whose laws he was safe, and provided against just such a contingency. I bought the documents from the owners before I left New York and when I ran the fox to earth in Brazil I claimed the papers as my property."

"By Jove! that was a sharp device."

"The law of course upheld my claim; with the proper officer I went to seize my man; he was desperate, being thus brought to bay, and showed fight. I had cautioned the officer to be on his guard, for I thought that there might be trouble. He was an arrogant boaster, despised my warning, and was killed at the first fire. The bullet was intended for me, but I dodged, and the officer got it. Then I grappled with my man, and although he fought like a tiger, succeeded in capturing him. I got my documents and the criminal was convicted of murder, and duly executed."

"Brand, you are a devil of a fellow!" the chief exclaimed. "If I were a rascal I should hate to have you strike my trail."

"I should do my best to make it lively and interesting for you," Brand placidly replied. "But now, superintendent, I want a little of your assistance. I landed from the English steamer this morning, and on my way up-town in a horse car some rascal stole my watch."

The chief lay back and laughed.

"Well, well!" he exclaimed, "if this isn't the richest joke of the season! The idea that a pick-pocket should select you for a subject to operate upon."

"And the worst of it is, that he succeeded in the operation; a handsome gold watch that I picked up in London at a bargain; cost me twenty-five pounds; and I haven't the remotest idea how the trick was done, excepting that as I stood on the rear platform waiting to get off, some fellow brushed past me rather rudely."

"Exactly, and that was just the time the trick was done. The two fellows stumbled up against you, you naturally elbowed them off, and a third fellow standing by your side snapped the watch off the ring."

"I guess you are 'about right, superintendent. I was in a sort of brown study at the time, or maybe I would have detected the trick."

"Give me a description, and I will do what I can for you by notifying the detectives and the pawn-brokers; but really, there isn't one chance out of a hundred for you to recover the property."

The description was given, and sent out by the superintendent; and then the official proceeded to explain to Brand about the matter in which he wished to enlist his services.

The man hunter listened attentively, and expressed his regrets when he learned of the death of Detective Brace.

"As good a man as I ever worked with," he observed.

"Yes, and you will perceive how difficult the task, when such a man as Brace not only failed to apprehend the murderer, but lost his life in the bargain."

"He must be avenged," Brand remarked, coldly and calmly, yet with a world of meaning in his tones.

"And you will undertake the job?"

"Right gladly."

Then the superintendent explained how deeply interested the mayor and governor had become in the matter.

"They will probably stand a big reward — as much as a thousand or two, maybe more, and then Juan Anchona will come down handsomely. Altogether, I shouldn't be surprised if you could pick up close to five thousand dollars if you succeed in trapping the murderer."

"The money is welcome enough, of course, although I am tolerably well provided, but I would undertake the work all the same if there wasn't a dollar up, for this mysterious assassin is no common stabber, and it is these superhuman villains that I delight to track. I believe I ought to have been born a bloodhound, for I take a fierce delight when I can get upon the track of such a magnificent rascal. There is no pleasure hunting down your common vulgar scoundrel; that is, not for a man like myself. If I cannot chase a big game, I prefer to remain idle."

"Well, judging from what has already occurred, this party will give you all the fun you want. But now, what do you think about the matter? You understand that as far as we can ascertain it was a woman who decoyed Brace to his death."

"Yes, but she is not the principal in the matter."

"You think not?"

"Oh, I feel sure of it; the woman never lived with nerve enough to commit these deeds."

"Women have done some pretty nervy things since the world began," the superintendent observed.

"Yes, but nothing of this sort."

"You forget the story of La Tour de Nesle."

"That was in a dark and barbarous age, despite the thin veneering of chivalry that covers it; besides there is no absolute proof that the tale is not a fiction. We cannot accept as literal truth all the stories that come down to us from days of yore. I have no doubt that the woman is an instrument, but not the master-mind. Chief, this fellow is one criminal picked out of ten thousand. He is a foreigner too, I think; his fantastic appearance, and the peculiar manner in which the death-wounds were inflicted, all go to prove that."

"Aha! do you think then that that blunderhead of a policeman did really see the man?"

"I have not the least doubt about it. He came up so quickly that the assassin was nearly surprised with the victim, and just had time to secrete himself behind the freight pile. Then, when he saw the policeman was not disposed to make much of a time, he came out and sauntered away."

"Yes, the fool supposed it was a case of natural death, but I say, how the deuce did the fellow manage to get the bodies to the public places where they were found without exciting attention, because it is clear to my mind that the men were not killed upon these spots?"

Brand shook his head.

"The conundrum is too much for you?"

"Yes, for the solving of that riddle would at once give a clew to the murderer, and that point is the one which requires to be carefully worked up."

The chief wanted to introduce Brand to the mayor and governor, but the detective begged to be excused, for he said he preferred to work in the dark.

"Do what you can for me in the way of the reward in case I trap the fellow," he observed in parting, "for money always comes in handy, and you know I work on the motto of 'no cure no pay.'"

Again they shook hands, and then Brand set out to prepare for his man-hunt.

The sleuth-hound possessed one great advantage; he had been absent so long from the city that all the new brood of rascals knew him not, and as he felt pretty certain that the mysterious assassin was no old offender, it was clear he would not be acquainted with his personal appearance.

Brand took up the lead that Brace had followed, reasoning that if Brade had succeeded in attracting the attention of the assassin he might do likewise but he intended the acquaintanceship should have a different ending.

CHAPTER XIII.

It was a terrible sea even for a strong man and an experienced swimmer to breast, for when the boat was overturned the storm was at its height and the waves were leaping about like angry demons.

The stranger, who had been hurled head-foremost into the water, soon rose to the surface, and despite the fact that he was sadly encumbered by the heavy cloak which he wore, struck out with lusty strokes for the overturned boat. A vivid flash of lightning just at this moment lit up the vast expanse of water, and the girl, who had risen to the surface about the same time, caught sight of her persecutor, and, as she did not lose her presence of mind in this dread extremity, Helena understood that he was trying to reach the boat, but as she was totally ignorant of the swimmer's art she could not hope to follow his example.

In her desperation she struck out wildly with her hands to keep from sinking beneath the surface of the wave. She was in the rear of the swimmer so that he did not perceive her.

Her clothing helped to buoy her up, but she was afraid that she would not be able to depend upon this aid for any length of time, and naught but a grave beneath the rolling billows seemed in store for her.

The lightning had died away and utter darkness reigned.

Alone, helpless upon the bosom of the raging water, could a poor mortal be placed in a more terrible plight?

In her great despair she called aloud, her voice mingling with the roar of the angry billows and the howling of the tempest.

"Oh, merciful God, our Father who art in heaven, save your poor handmaiden in this her hour of peril!"

And the Great Creator, the only friend of the orphan and the helpless, deigned to listen to the heartfelt prayer, and sent assistance.

Her hands encountered a solid substance floating upon the surface of the waves; with the energy born of despair she grasped it.

It was the broken mast with the sail still attached, but the action of the billows had rolled it around the spar so that it formed an efficient support.

"Oh, Heaven, I thank thee for this timely aid!" the girl murmured in gratitude, as she wound her arms around the floating buoy.

And now, as if satisfied with the mischief which had been wrought, there was a lull in the tempest; no more did the lightning's flash illuminate the scene; the darkness was intense, so that Helena was unable to ascertain whether her persecutor had been able to reach the overturned boat, which had been floating keel upward, or had succumbed to the fury of the waves.

In either case, though, it mattered not to her for she was safe from his attacks.

There was some of the cordage still attached to the spar, floating loosely from it; this, with really wonderful forethought, she wound around her person, so that if her physical strength failed she might be supported by that novel life-preserver.

Although not much acquainted with the sea, having always resided in an inland town, yet, from what she had read, she thought in time the spar would be carried by the action of the waves to the beach, and and then, if the surf was not so terrible as to beat the life out of her when she was flung upon the strand, she would be able to escape without serious injury.

The girl's surmise was right; the spar was carried by the rolling billows in toward the shore, and, as the darkness began to lighten up a little, she could distinguish the white line of the surf where it spent its fury upon the sandy beach.

Helena was both strong of heart and stout in limb, and had been careful to husband all her strength, for she understood that the supreme effort must be made when the surf flung her upon the land. She must be prepared to escape the undertow, which would inevitably drag her back into the raging billows if she was not careful.

So, as she gradually drew near the land, she released herself from the ropes which she had wound around her body, prepared to abandon the spar when the necessity became urgent for her so to do.

Nearer and nearer she came; she fancied once or twice that her feet touched bottom, so shallow had become the water, and the white line of the raging surf, pouring in upon the beach with a roar like the report of a mammoth battery of artillery, could plainly be distinguished, notwithstanding the darkness that veiled the face of nature.

And now again and again her feet touched bottom as she surged in toward the beach and then was borne out again by the force of the restless waters; but although she tried with all her strength, it was impossible for her to retain her footing, so powerful being the swell of the billows.

At last, by an unusually powerful wave she was carried on its foamy crest high up on the beach.

She felt that the critical time had come. She relinquished her hold upon the spar, which had served her so well, suffering it to be carried away by the retreating wave, dug her nails into the sand and held on for dear life.

The wave upon whose crest she had floated was an unusually high one, and so its undertow was not as strong as otherwise it would have been.

The retreating water made a determined effort to force the girl from her hold, as though reluctant to give up its prey, but was not powerful enough to accomplish its purpose.

The instant the water relaxed its grasp upon her, and went roaring as if in sullen rage back to the stormy main, the girl, summoning all her strength, rose to her feet; but she was so weak from the effects of the hardship which she had undergone, that she could not walk, and the moment she attempted to move forward her limbs gave way beneath her and she sunk forward upon her face again.

And then came another mighty wave thundering upon the beach, one even more powerful than that which had carried the girl to land.

Again Helena dug her nails into the strand, and struggled against the power of the water; again she succeeded in resisting its force, and then, when the breaker retreated, warned by experience, she did not attempt to rise, but crawled on hands and knees away from the line of the surf.

It was a slow and painful progress, for the girl was weak from exhaustion, her brain in a whirl, and she had all she could do to keep from relapsing into insensibility.

Desperately she struggled against the faintness which was creeping over her, but resolute as was her determined will, she was not able to conquer nature; the strain upon her strength had been too much, and before she had crept a dozen feet higher upon the beach she succumbed to fatigue and fainted dead away.

Although some distance from the spot where she had first landed, she was not yet out of danger.

She had been cast upon the beach by the last wave of the ebb tide; now it had turned to flood, and was encroaching steadily upon the beach, gaining inch by inch.

The girl lay in her stupor perfectly helpless, and the restless water, like a malignant demon, gradually and surely approached her.

The beach was quite a level one at the point upon which the girl was cast, and although she had crawled some distance from where she had first landed, she had barely gained a foot in height.

Along this part of the coast the tide rises about six feet, making, consequently, about a foot an hour, and so, within a very short time the angry breakers were again thundering close to the feet of the girl.

Twenty minutes more and most surely she would have been wrapped in the embraces of the stormy waves, and in her helpless condition such a thing would have been the prelude to certain death.

But it was not fated to be.

Through the darkness, along the beach, came a glimmering light — the light proceeded from a lantern borne by one dark form, while another followed in the rear, plodding over the sand, with their eyes fixed eagerly upon the edge of the breakers.

It was a man and woman, roughly dressed, and with coarse, ugly, repulsive features.

In one hand the man carried the lantern and in the other a boat-hook; the woman also was equipped with a similar tool.

Night prowlers were these two, relics of the old pirates of Barnegat, the wreckers who, if report speaks true, in the old days had scant mercy upon the unfortunate souls possessed of worldly goods, unlucky enough to be cast upon their dangerous coast.

"Hello, hello!" cried the man, as his eyes fell upon the form of the girl, "here is something that may pay us for our trouble!"

"Ay, ay," responded the woman, hurrying forward, and peering in eager curiosity upon the girl.

"Pears like as if thar had bin a wrack somewhar's 'long the coast, but I hain't seen any stuff come ashore."

"Is she dead?" queried the old woman.

The man knelt down and placed his hand upon the wrist of the helpless girl.

"No, she bean't; she's alive, but I reckon she's had a mighty close shave of it. Anyhow, if we hadn't happened to come along, them breakers would 'a had a hold on her mighty soon, and then she would have been a goner, for sure."

"She's a lady; jest see what little white hands, and she's got a rare face, too."

"She ain't got much jewelry, as far as I kin see," the man observed, examining the girl with wolfish eyes.

"Oh, she'll be worth a heap of jewelry to us," the woman concluded. "Lay hold on her, old man, and let's drag her up out of the reach of this water. This will be a rare haul for us, I'll go bail."

CHAPTER XIV.

THE surmise of the mysterious stranger, the abductor of the girl, in regard to the young sailor having a great deal of the bull-dog about him, was correct, as he undoubtedly would have admitted if he could have followed in Blakely's footsteps and watched his movements when he set out to discover what had become of the girl.

The sailor had thought the matter over carefully. From the little he had seen of the unknown he had come to the conclusion that he was not much of a mariner, and he felt tolerably certain that no one but an old and experienced sailor would succeed in safely running down the Jersey coast in such a boat and in such a gale. The chances were good, he thought, that the boat would not be able to live in such a sea, nor to make a landing without capsizing; in either event it was possible that the occupants of the craft might be able to reach the shore, particularly if the attempt was made near one of the life-saving stations and they were aided by the coast patrol. But the night had been so dark that it would hardly have been possible for the patrolmen to distinguish the boat until she was right on the beach, and only from some one of the patrol happening to be near the spot when the boat came ashore could assistance be had.

There was a bare possibility that the two might have escaped the perils of the night, but the chances that they had perished were much greater. This was the riddle he must solve.

Blakely set about his task in a workmanlike manner.

From a friend of sporting proclivities, who was particularly interested in horseflesh, he procured an excellent saddle-nag, and with the horse he took his way by boat to the Jersey coast.

The sailor was well acquainted with the lay of the land, as at various times he had visited the regions during the summer season.

From the manner in which the boat sped away before the wind, after getting around the point of Sandy Hook, Blakely calculated that there would not be any particular danger of a capsize until the skipper undertook to put the boat about in order to return; then, unless he handled the craft carefully and in a sailor-like manner, the maneuver would result in an upset.

Blakely's plan was to mount his horse and ride down along the beach, inquiring of every one he met if they knew anything of a small boat containing a man and woman which had come ashore during the night. The young sailor had set about his task so promptly that he had managed to get upon the ground on the afternoon of the very day that the City of Chester had made her berth.

Diligently inquired the young man, but not a particle of information did he gain until he came to the collection of fishermen's huts known as "Galilee," just above Long Branch.

A fishing boat, with four sturdy sons of the brine, had just come to land, and were occupied in putting their finny spoil into baskets when Blakely rode up.

"I am in search of a boat that was blown around Sandy Hook last night, during the gale, with a man and woman in it," he said. "Have you heard anything of a boat coming ashore anywhere along here?"

"A small keel-boat with a sail rigged into her?" asked the oldest of the fishermen, a white-bearded veteran.

"Yes; painted green without and white within."

"Like that 'ere boat up yonder?" and the fisherman pointed to a space between two of the houses where a small craft had been hauled up out of the water.

It was the identical boat, Blakely was sure, but the sail and nearly all of the mast were gone, only a few inches of the latter remaining, the jagged end giving plain proof that it had been snapped by some violent gust of wind.

"Yes; that is the boat, but what became of the people?"

"Did you say that there was two on board on her?"

"Yes; a man and a woman."

"Wa-al, I don't know anything 'bout the woman, but the man is all right."

"No young girl with him?" cried Blakely, who cared nothing for the man, and would not have grieved if he had been told the scoundrel had perished in the storm.

"Nary gal! I reckon she must have gone under when the boat upset."

"She upset, then?"

"Yes, I'll tell you how it was; you know thar was considerable of a storm last night?"

Blakely nodded assent.

"And from the way the wind blew, I reckoned we were going to have a pretty big tide, and it kinder worried me, 'cos I thought the boys hadn't hauled the boats fur enough up-on the beach, so 'bout four o'clock I got up, dressed myself, and went out to see how things looked. The storm was 'bout over then, but thar was a dreadful heavy swell hammering in; it was pesky dark, but I managed to make out that thar was something a-driving in toward the land through the surf, and after a time I saw that it was a boat, bottom upward, and thar seemed to be a man clinging to it.

"I gave the alarm at once, and the boys come tumbling out. We got a boat into the water — and it was risky work, for the breakers were as big as a house — pulled out, and diskivered that it was a man, sure enough, and the poor cuss was about gone; he couldn't have held on much longer; why, he hadn't strength to speak when we got him into the boat. If it a-hadn't been for us, I tell yer, nothing but his dead body would have ever come on this hyar beach, for the surf would have pounded out what little life remained."

"But you saved him by your timely aid, and he is alive?"

"Oh, I'll bet yes! up to the house yonder," and the fisherman pointed to the nearest hut. "After we got him inter the house I poured about a pint of whisky down him which kinder braced him up, and then we rolled him in blankets, and when we set off on our fishing trip this morning, he felt 'pretty well, I thank you!'"

The blood leaped more quickly within the veins of the young man when he thought that the perpetrator of the outrage, which had evidently cost the unfortunate girl her life, was so near at hand. If she had found a grave beneath the rolling green waters, he, the actual cause of her death was still living — still able to pay the penalty that an outraged law could exact for the crime.

"In yonder house?"

"Yes, mister."

"Rather tall, slender fellow, dark complexion, long, black hair, and speaks with a slight accent, like a foreigner?"

"Wall, no, mister. I reckon you are barking up the wrong tree," the fisherman replied. "This hyar cuss don't fill that bill at all. He's a leetle dark in the face, not quite so white as you are, but his hair is short, instead of long, and he speaks as good United States talk as either you or me."

Then it suddenly occurred to Blakely that the long hair and the accent might have been a part of a disguise assumed by the unknown for the purpose of concealing his identity.

"Well, I only saw him for a few minutes, and it is possible that I may be wrong in regard to these particulars," he observed.

"In course I don't know nothing 'bout that," the fisherman remarked. "All I know is what the feller looks like that I hauled out of the sea, 'bout as near death as a man could come and yet live to tell of it."

As the veteran made this remark, the conversation of the sailors regarding the vampire came back to Blakely, and he could not help thinking that the vampire, despite his supernatural character, had had a pretty narrow squeeze for his life.

"I have probably made a mistake about his personal appearance, but that is natural under the circumstances," Blakely said. "I've not the least doubt that it is the man I mean, for that certainly is the boat. I am a sailor, and not apt to forget a craft that my eyes have once seen."

"It is rather an odd little egg-shell, anyway; I reckon a man must be rather keerless of his life for to trust himself in such a boat as that outside of Sandy Hook in a gale like was a-blowing last night," the fisherman remarked. "I reckon the best hundred-dollar gold piece that was ever shoved out of the mint wouldn't have been any temptation for me to do any sich foolish thing! The man must have been crazy for to do it, and carry a gal along with him, too!"

"Crazy!" the fisherman struck the key-note when he uttered that word, and the thought occurred to Blakely that the stranger, by some wild words or actions, had given occasion for the man to form this opinion.

"Does there seem to be anything the matter with him — does he talk or act strangely?" he asked.

"Oh, no, he's all right, although he must have gone through enough to have turned almost any man's head inside out; I tell you what it is, stranger, it war a thousand to one ag'in his gitting safe to the shore last night. Another thirty minutes would have settled his hash! If it hadn't been for the whisky, I reckon he would have been a goner, any-how."

"I'd like to see him, if you haven't any objection."

"Not at all. Come right along with me."

The fisherman led the way, and Blakely followed, feeling sure that in a few moments he would solve one mystery at least.

CHAPTER XV.

Anita Anchona was a pretty girl; there wasn't the least doubt about that, as everybody admitted. She was rather below the medium size, a pronounced brunette, with sparkling black eyes, beautiful hair of the same hue, soft as silk, and as lustrous as the plumage of a raven.

In disposition she was lively and agreeable, a perfect lady in every respect, although rather disposed to be outspoken in her views.

For a girl that from early childhood had been brought up to understand that she was the only daughter and, consequently, the sole heir of a man worth millions, she was remarkably free from all pride and ostentation.

In fact, at the fashionable boarding-school where she had been educated, she was a source of wonder to both teachers and pupils, the majority of whom were rather disposed to bow down and worship the golden calf, for she was as unassuming as the poorest girl in the place, and many a time, when some companion had allowed an envious expression to escape, Anita would reply:

"Why, girls, I am not any better off than the rest of you, as far as I know; people all say that my pa is dreadfully rich, and I know that we live in a beautiful house and have horses and carriages and such things, but as far as I am concerned, it doesn't do me much good. I do not dress any better than the rest, and I am sure that my allowance of pin-money is ridiculously small, for I manage to get rid of it long before the next quarter is due.

"Some of you imagine, no doubt, that all I have to do when I want money is to write to pa and he sends me a blank check, so that I can fill it out with whatever sum suits my fancy, but I tell you girls it isn't that way at all.

"My pa only allows me five hundred dollars a year, one hundred of which is paid to me in quarterly installments, and the balance I draw upon to dress myself.

"Now, girls, four hundred dollars a year isn't a very large sum for a millionaire's daughter to spend.

"Pa makes me a present of a very handsome dress once in a while, or a piece of jewelry, but not often, for he says there is no telling what may happen in this uncertain world; and as many a man, fully as good as he is in every respect, supports a family upon the sum he allows me, I ought to have wit enough to make it supply my wants.

"Then, too, he says wealth is a peculiar thing: money takes to itself wings and flies away, you know; I may be a poor man's wife, one of these days, and if I have always been used to taking care of my money, I will know how to get along."

This was the way in which Juan Anchona had brought up the girl, and the result was she had arrived at the age of twenty-one as natural and as unspoiled by her position as any mechanic's daughter in the land.

Anita was sitting by one of the windows in the parlor, looking idly out upon the street, the last new book upon her lap, when the millionaire entered the room.

There was a troubled expression upon the face of Anchona. The miscarriage of his plans in regard to the girl whom he had been at the trouble of bringing across the ocean annoyed him; it was a small matter, apparently, and yet the millionaire seemed to take it more to heart than anything that had occurred in years, although there had been many an up and down to the path which Anchona had followed.

"Anita, I want to have a little serious talk with you," he said, taking a chair and seating himself opposite to the girl.

"Yes, sir," she replied, surprised by the expression upon his face, for it showed that a heavy weight rested upon his mind.

"I will come at once to the point. What do you think of this young gentleman who has been paying you so much attention — Mr. Lee?" he questioned.

"Really, father, to answer you frankly, I must say I don't exactly know."

"Well, but isn't it about time you made up your mind? He has been paying you attention for quite a long while."

"Yes, sir, I know it."

"And can't you tell how you feel toward him in regard to the matter?"

"Oh, yes, sir, I can do that easily enough," the girl replied, quickly. "I like him and I don't like him. He is very agreeable, a perfect gentleman, very entertaining, for he has been almost everywhere and knows something of almost everything. As a pleasant companion he is far superior to any of the other gentlemen with whom I am acquainted, but when I come to look upon him in the light of a suitor — as a man who is to be my husband, and with whom I must spend the rest of my days, then a doubt creeps in. I do not know exactly any reason why I should doubt — why I should not be happy with him, but I have a strange sort of feeling in regard to the matter that I cannot account for on any reasonable grounds. I like him as a friend, and yet some secret instinct seems to tell me that as a husband I should not like him."

"Is there any other gentleman?" Anchona asked, with a searching glance at the girl's face.

"Oh. no, sir!" Truth itself dwelt in Anita's words, and the old man accepted the statement without question.

"Well, I did not know but you had seen some one else who pleased you better."

"No, sir, I like Mr. Lee as well as any gentleman that I have ever met: in fact, I am pretty sure I like him better, that is, I enjoy myself more in his company. Of course, knowing your views in the matter, I have endeavored to look upon him as a man who would one day be my lord and master, but somehow I cannot accustom myself to viewing him in that light. I do not feel toward him as a girl should feel toward the man who is one day to be all in all to her."

"That is strange."

"Yes, it is very odd; but it is possible that I do not rightly understand the nature of the feeling which is called love. All that I know about the matter is what I have gained from books, and from the confidences reposed in me by some of my schoolmates. At all events I do not feel toward Mr. Lee, or anybody else either, as the heroines of the novels feel toward their lovers, or as my girl friends feel toward the gentlemen to whom they are engaged. It is possible that I am an odd girl — everybody at school used to say I was — and that I am not capable of experiencing this passion, which is called love. It is certain that I never have yet."

"I do not think that you are in any important particular different from the rest of your sex," the old gentleman observed. "When the time comes for you to love, you will most certainly feel the passion, although it is possible that with your strange notions you may never experience the passionate love which is the stock in trade of the novelist. If you like the gentleman well enough to marry him, the love may come afterward."

"Yes; that is what all my lady friends say when they attempt to joke me about Mr. Lee. When I tell them that I really do not love him, they all laugh, as if they do not believe me, and exclaim, 'Oh, but you will, dear, after you are married.'"

"Anita, I do not want to attempt to influence you in this matter at all," M. Anchona remarked, "because I think every girl ought to be free to choose for herself, but as far as I know, the gentleman would make you a good husband. He comes of a fine family, is a man of means, a pleasant fellow personally, and I think he is attracted to you solely by your own gifts and not from the fact that you are my daughter, and he expects you will inherit my property when I depart from this life."

"Oh, I do not think he is a fortune-hunter, father; he certainly does not appear like one."

"And if he is one and weds you, Anita, under the idea that you will inherit my money, he will be sadly disappointed."

The girl looked surprised.

"The time has come, Anita, when a secret that concerns you closely must be revealed. I have always acted like a kind and indulgent parent to you?"

"Always, dear father!" and she knelt by his side.

"And yet I am not your father."

"Not any father?"

"No, my dear girl, nor any relative. Your father and mother died when you were a baby. Heaven never saw fit to bless myself and wife with a child; chance threw you in our way and we adopted and reared you as our own; and that is something that neither myself nor wife ever regretted, for you have always been a dutiful, loving child; and now for the reason why you will not be my heiress. The greater part of the money that stands in my name is really not mine. I am but a trustee for another. My own fortune, although a goodly sum, does not entitle me to the name of millionaire. I shall leave you comfortably well off, but the man who marries you, expecting to get a million or more, will be sadly disappointed. I thought if you seriously reflected upon wedding Mr. Lee, I had better see him and explain how matters stand. The rightful heir of the money will doubtless soon claim it, and if any untoward accident should interfere to prevent the party from coming forward, I should feel bound to turn the money over to some deserving charities, for I could not conscientiously retain it."

"Perhaps it would be as well for you to speak to Mr. Lee, and then if he persists in his suit it will be proof that he is attracted by myself alone."

"Very well, I will set about the matter at once," and the old gentleman departed, leaving the girl full of wonder.

CHAPTER XVI.

WHILE Brand had decided to try about the same game which had resulted so fatally to the murdered detective, yet he proceeded in a slightly different manner. Brace had gone in for a big display, swaggered about considerably for the purpose of making a decided impression so as to attract the notice of the bird whom he desired to snare.

This was Brand's idea also, but he did not take the trouble to disguise himself. He had been absent from New York for some time; the hot sun of the tropics had bronzed his complexion; he had allowed his mustache to grow and sported a small chin-piece, after the foreign fashion, so that no one but an intimate acquaintance, like the superintendent of police, would be apt to recognize him.

As Brace had selected the Fifth Avenue Hotel for his headquarters, Brand did likewise. He registered as Antonio Molina, Rio Janeiro, Brazil, and took occasion whenever opportunity offered to display a big roll of bills, all apparently of large denominations, which he carried, carelessly done up in a wad, in an inside breast-pocket of his coat.

Brand, being possessed of a noble, commanding presence, well calculated to inspire respect at the first glance, made a most decided impression on everybody whom he encountered, and all of the *attaches* of the hotel set him down as one of the Brazilian diamond kings of whose wealth New Yorkers have a high opinion. During his sojourn in South America, the detective had become familiar with the language of that country and could converse quite freely in Spanish.

So completely did Brand impress the hotel people with the idea that he was possessed of "stacks of money," and was rather ignorant of the ways of the great city, particularly one so full of rascals as the metropolis of the New World, and all without putting him to the necessity of boasting about who and what he was, that three or four of them took upon themselves the task of warning the supposed stranger to be more careful in regard to displaying the money he carried.

Brand thanked them for the caution, but replied in the calm tone of a man who knew not the meaning of the word fear, that whether in the wilds of his native pampas, or in Gotham's crowded town, he felt amply able to defend himself either from open or secret foes, whether his valuables or life were threatened.

The detective played the part of a rich foreigner, who had come to New York expressly for amusement, to perfection. His tall form was seen in the public places; all the leading theaters were honored by his presence, nor did he neglect the gilded saloons where the bloods of New York, and the excitement seekers from afar, meet to try their luck at beating the smooth and oily gamblers at their own game.

With the most superb indifference Brand won or lost his money, always hazarding a goodly sum, as became a man to whom a thousand or two was a mere trifle.

Two weeks went by and not a single bite did the detective have. Even the lesser rogues, the confidence men and bunco operators fought shy of the prince-like foreigner, although not having the slightest suspicion that he was otherwise than what he seemed; but there was something about the man that awed them. No doubt he would turn out a rich prize if he could be entrapped, but they were afraid to run the risk, for the chances seemed to them to be those that accompany a tiger hunt; if the chase was not successful there was danger that the game would turn and rend the hunter. Brand began to believe that the attempt to entrap the secret assassin would prove a failure.

"Either the fellow has given up business, or else he has penetrated my design and is going to keep quiet until I give up the chase, but if that is his intention, he'll have to wait a deuced long while," the detective mused.

That afternoon one of the hotel clerks, whom he met in the hall and stopped to converse with for awhile, called his attention to a lady who happened to pass at the moment.

"By the bye, Mr. Molina, that is a country woman of yours," he said; "she is a Brazilian, and from Rio Janeiro, too, Miss Marita Madriea. She is stopping here, waiting for the coming of her father, who has been across the water on business. She's high-toned, I tell you! Just notice her diamonds! Magnificent, ain't they? Well, I should smile!"

Brand took a good look at the lady, who was now descending the stairs; from where he was standing he commanded a view of her face. She was rather tall, with a fine figure and impressive features. It could not be really termed a handsome face; the features, though regular, were rather course; but she was stylish-looking, a woman who would be apt to attract favorable attention everywhere.

"She's a stunner, ain't she?" the clerk continued; "a perfect lady, too. I had quite an agreeable conversation with her in the parlor yesterday. I'm the best hand at her language in the house, you know."

"Does she speak English?"

"Oh, yes, and with a very slight accent, too, but of course it is pleasant for her to meet some one who can converse with her in her own language. I mentioned the fact that you were also from Rio, and she said she had noticed you in the dining-room, and from your appearance conjectured that you were not an American; she inquired your name, but did not remember ever meeting you at home when I told her where it was."

Brand thought it would be deuced funny if she had remembered either himself or his appellation.

"The lady is a stranger to me, but then you must remember that Rio is a big city."

"Oh, yes; but I say, wouldn't you like me to make you acquainted with her? She intimated to me that it would be agreeable to her."

"I shall be delighted to have the honor," Brand replied.

The detective made it a rule to always make the acquaintance of everybody that he could, for in his peculiar business there was no telling when the most unlikely person might turn out to be of great importance. And he thought that while he was waiting for the game to walk into the trap, he might as well amuse himself by making all the agreeable acquaintances possible.

"You'll enjoy her conversation, I'm sure," the clerk remarked. "She's a really brilliant girl — been everywhere, and seen almost everything. She's style all the way through, and there isn't the least bit of nonsense about her, no stuck-up pride, although I don't doubt that she is just rolling in money! I suppose, anyway, that down in Brazil you are not so deuced particular — don't stand so much upon ceremony as we do here."

"We are less formal, I presume."

"I guess it is that way in all hot-weather countries."

"I suppose it is due to the climate. The southern people are not so much given to ceremony as the dwellers in the north."

"I will tell her the first chance I get, and I've no doubt she will want me to bring you up to her parlors. I tell you, senor, she lives in style. She's got about the best suit of apartments we have in the house. Any one can see from the way she spends her money that she must have one of those Brazilian diamond mines to draw upon, or else she would never be able to stand it."

Brand again expressed the pleasure it would give him to become acquainted with the lady, and the clerk passed on.

Late that afternoon, just as the detective was finishing his dinner, the clerk came up, and Brand guessed from the expression of satisfaction that appeared upon his jolly face, that he had succeeded in his design.

"It's all right," he said, leaning on Brand's chair and whispering in his ear. "I've fixed the matter. She said she would be delighted to make the acquaintance of any gentlemen from Rio; so, as soon as you get through, I will carry you up, and in honor of the occasion, I'm going to stand a bottle of the best wine that there is in the cellar."

"All right, I will do justice to it if the lady doesn't," Brand answered.

And so, about an hour later, the detective was ushered by the hotel official into the reception room of Miss Marita Madriea.

The lady was richly attired, wore most magnificent jewelry, and conducted herself with an ease and grace that gave ample proof she had been accustomed to the best society.

After they had conversed together for some ten minutes, a grinning African made his appearance, bearing a tray upon which was a bottle of champagne and three glasses.

The clerk explained that he had taken the liberty of ordering the wine.

"Sort of a surprise party, you know," he added.

Miss Madriea laughed, shook her finger at the clerk and declared he was "a horrid fellow!" but it was plain that she was pleased with the attention.

"There's some dust in the glasses," she said, "uncork the wine, please, while I wipe them out."

Then, while the clerk proceeded to show his skill with the corkscrew, the lady took the glasses under the chandelier, and, turning her back to the two gentlemen, apparently proceeded to wipe the glasses with her handkerchief, but in reality she took a small vial, containing a colorless liquid, from her bosom, and with noiseless rapidity poured a few drops in the bottom of two of the glasses.

This act was performed so quickly and so skillfully that neither of the gentlemen had the slightest suspicion.

Then when the wine was poured out she managed to arrange it so that the glass which had not been tampered with fell to her.

"Now, gentlemen, I will give you a toast!" she exclaimed. "Success to all our wishes!"

CHAPTER XVII.

"Bravo! Miss Madriea, that is a most excellent toast, and I will drink it with a great deal of pleasure," the clerk exclaimed, and although Brand merely bowed and smiled, he thought it would be a good thing for him if the toast could be realized.

Merrily the three pledged each other, and then drained their glasses.

Brand drank without a suspicion that there was anything wrong, for so shrewdly had the trick been worked that it would have required more than human knowledge to detect it.

But the moment the detective swallowed the wine and resumed his seat, following the example of the hotel clerk, he became conscious that he had been "dosed" — that there had been a drug administered in the wine, and he knew well enough what it was, too, for no stranger was he to the peculiar way in which it worked upon the brain.

The effect produced upon the clerk was almost instantaneous, and was really wonderful.

He was occupying an easy-chair, and as the subtle drug coursed through his veins, he leaned back, totally regardless of the presence of the lady, and half closed his eyes in a sleepy way.

"Well, 'pon my word if that isn't the nicest wine I ever got hold of since I knew what wine was, you bet! Splendid wine — I think I could drink a couple of bottles of that wine, all alone by myself — splendid that is — I think — I think — that — I — dunno exactly what I think, but — bully — wine --" and then, with a sort of hoarse groan, the clerk relaxed into insensibility.

Brand, too, had lolled back in his chair, his eyes half-closed, and a dazed, vacant sort of look upon his face; but it was evident the drug had not mastered him so completely as it had his companion.

Either he had not taken so powerful a dose, or else having a stronger head was more able to resist the bewildering influence.

The woman was quick to discover that though the drug had worked to a charm upon the hotel official, rendering him completely insensible to all that was passing around, yet Brand, although deprived of muscular power, was yet conscious of what was going on.

The woman, who had also sunk back into an easy-chair after drinking, now rose to her feet, with the look of a demon upon her face.

She came close to Brand and glared into his face with eyes that fairly seemed to blaze with vivid light.

"You understand me when I speak?" she exclaimed.

Brand seemed to attempt to reply, but when he opened his mouth, he was like a man whose tongue has been removed; all he could do was to articulate some discordant sounds.

"If you cannot speak, nod!"

But Brand plainly could no more do the one than the other, for when he attempted to obey the command, the best he could do was to move his eyes.

This she instantly noticed.

"Ah, well, it doesn't matter," she remarked. "I see you understand what I am saying, and this is all I care about. You must have a head of iron to take such a dose and yet be able to understand what is going on around you while your muscular powers are so affected that you are not able to lift a finger."

Again there was a movement of Brand's eyes, and a light shone therein, which, when it was noticed by the woman, caused her to burst into a peal of laughter.

"Oho, my stolid-faced, lion-hearted comrade!" she cried. "You would make short work of me if you were not bound hard and fast as if by an iron chain! You are a wonderful man — there are many wonderful men in the world, and yet there are very few of them who succeed in going through life without, at some time or other, happening to meet their master. You have met yours now, as I have no doubt you would frankly confess if you were able to speak. It is strange, though, when one comes to think of it, the difference that must exist between you and this shallow-brained idiot," and she pointed, contemptuously, to the clerk. "He is good to remain in this state of stupor for five or ten hours, while I have no doubt you would fully recover in an hour or two, if nature was allowed to have her way."

There was a world of menace in the intonation which the woman gave to the closing sentence of the speech, and Brand, who plainly comprehended exactly what she meant, possibly would not have been able to repress a shudder if he could have moved a muscle.

"But for an hour or two, despite your strength — despite your wonderful skill and courage, you will be so helpless that a child could slay you without the least trouble. Both the time and the place, too, are propitious for such a deed. We are not liable to be interrupted, but to make assurance doubly sure, I will lock the door and remove the key."

And by the time she had finished speaking the act was performed. Then she returned, drew up a chair and sat down in it, facing Brand, and so near him that by simply stretching out her hand she could touch his breast.

"Now, then, before the last act of this delightful comedy begins, permit me to say a few words, and explain why it is that I have taken upon myself to play a leading part and turn the comedy into a tragedy."

No movement on the part of Brand, but in his eyes a peculiar expression, a far-away look, which puzzled the woman for a moment.

"Has the drug affected him differently from what it should? Is he dying?" she questioned.

It was little wonder the woman got this impression, for Brand looked far more like a corpse than aught else.

"Do you understand me?"

There was a faint quiver of the eyelids; apparently the only way in which the man could give assurance that he was alive.

"It is very strange that he should be affected in this way," she murmured. "The drug has evidently thrown him into a trance-like state, rendered him incapable of moving, and yet he is able to see and understand all that is passing around him. It is really a marvelous case! But now to business without loss of time."

"Do you know me, sir?"

Again the movement of the eyelids.

"You do not, of course, but I know you, Antonio Molina. This is a very good name, and you are from Rio, too," she added, "but you are not a native of that city, not even a resident, and the name Carlton Brand, the detective, would become you much better than the other. You are playing a bold and skillful game, my hero, and yet you were foolish to believe that such a man as yourself could be forgotten in so short a time. Oh, no, Brand, you man-hunter, you have run down too many poor fellows — have made yourself too terrible a name to easily pass from the memory of men. You were an old friend of Brace, and when you returned from abroad and found that the hunter had been caught in his own snare — the engineer hoist by his own petard — you determined to try your luck. You would discover and bring to justice the unknown who laughed to scorn all the efforts of the police, and yet with all your wisdom you could do no better than to attempt to play the same game which had resulted so fatally to your old-time pal, and the end is, you are snared fully as easily as he was!

"Oh, it's a rare joke, if you look at it in the right way," the woman cried, with an outburst of merriment that sounded really fiendish. "To think that you, Carlton Brand

— Brand, the renowned! — should be the dupe of so shallow a trick! And you walked into the trap without the slightest suspicion! Brace was caught in exactly the same way, excepting that I allowed him to make my acquaintance on the street, lured him to my den, and there drugged and killed him. I did not dare to try that game on you, for, warned by the fate of your brother detective, you would have been a fool indeed if you had not been upon your guard, but thanks to the good-nature of this meddling donkey of a clerk, the trick was worked to perfection.

"Brand, I do not doubt that you must have been very near death a hundred times in the course of your life of adventures, but never since you came into this world of sorrow have you been as near as you are at this moment.

"You seek the assassin who slays the victims with a single blow, piercing the heart — the secret slayer who has covered up the track so well that no one has yet succeeded in gaining the slightest clew. But you -you, my bold and vigilant Brand, are more successful than the rest, for now you are face to face with the perpetrator of these deeds of darkness. Look well at me — feast your eyes with the sight of the face that you hoped to place behind a prison's bars!

"Do you doubt my words? If so, behold the weapon with which the deeds were done!"

In the coils of her lustrous, jet-black hair shone a diamond cross, a beautiful ornament, fully three inches long.

She plucked it out, and lo! the pin, which had been hidden in her hair, was a polished steel dagger, nearly six inches in length, and a little larger round than an ordinary knitting-needle.

She brandished the weapon before the face of the detective, while her eyes seemed to glow with unnatural light.

"It is a toy, and yet it has drunk the heart's blood of many a strong man, and hurled him before his time into the cold, damp grave!" she cried. "And now, Carlton Brand, it is your turn, and after you, this miserable fool, although he is barely worth the killing, but I crave blood — I cannot have too much of it; if I cannot get plunder, I can, at least, slake my thirst for gore! One blow is all I need, Brand, one single blow, and I will pierce your heart at the very first stroke, for I know exactly where to strike. Now!"

And with determined arm she drove the dagger into his breast, right at the heart.

CHAPTER XVIII.

BLAKELY dismounted from his horse the moment the fisherman's words had revealed to him that the abductor of the girl was near at hand; no need to fasten the animal, for he was too well trained to stir from the spot.

The fisherman was met upon the threshold by his wife, a matronly-looking dame, with a good, honest face.

"Well, mother, how's the man?" the fisherman asked.

"All right, I guess; he wanted a cup of coffee a few minutes ago, and I made him a good strong one, which he took with a relish."

"That was right; thar's nothing like a cup of strong coffee to put life into a man after he has been out exposed to the weather," the veteran observed.

"This gentleman has come to see him, mother; he thinks he knows him, least ways he knows the boat, and as the craft is the one be is arter, I reckon the man is, too."

"You'll find him jest where you left him, up-stairs in the hack room."

"Come right up with me, sir," said the man, leading the way to the upper story.

Blakely followed, while the woman brought up the rear.

"In this room, sir," and the old salt opened the door, which was fastened only by a simple latch.

A step more and Blakely would be face to face with the abductor; the blood in his veins fairly tingled at the thought, and, involuntarily, his hands clinched, anxious to take the ruffian by the throat.

He crossed the threshold, and, as he did so, an exclamation of amazement came from the lips of the fisherman, who was some three steps in advance.

The apartment was empty.

There was the humble bed, with its coarse covering, the impression still visible where the man had been lying, but the man himself was not to be seen.

"Hello, mother! I thought you said the critter was in here?"

"So he was — only a minit ago," and the woman looked around her with a bewildered air, as if asking where on earth her guest had gone.

"He must have come down-stairs without your seeing him."

"Sakes alive! he couldn't," she declared, in answer to her husband. "It war only a minit ago I brought up his coffee and he sot on the edge of the bed while he drank it; I axed him how he felt, and he allowed he felt pretty near all right; then I went down-stairs, and I've been in the room ever since. I didn't stir out of it, and he couldn't have come down-stairs without my seeing him — that is jest as sure as were all standing here!"

And as the stairs led into the lower apartment, it was clear the woman was correct.

There was a small window at the back of the room. Blakely advanced to it and looked out. Right under the window was a shed-like extension, and the moment the sailor saw it the mystery of the man's disappearance was revealed. It was perfectly easy, even for a child, to get out of the window to the shed and then descend to the ground.

"This is the way your man went," he remarked.

"Thunder! what on earth possessed the critter to git out of the winder?" the fisherman queried.

"He needn't 'a bin afeered for to come down the stairs. We wasn't a-going for to charge 'im anything," the good wife exclaimed, quite angry to think the stranger should have behaved so unhandsomely after all her trouble. "We're Christian folks, and we wouldn't have thought of taking-money for helping a fellow being that we had pulled out of the sea — drat the man! what kind of critters did he take us to be?" Blakely had guessed the solution to the riddle, although he did not take the trouble to enlighten the fisherman and his wife. The sandy track along which he had journeyed was in full sight of the window; the fellow was probably looking out when he rode by, caught sight of him, anticipated his errand, and proceeded to get out of the way as speedily as possible.

"Durned if I like this kind of business," grumbled the man. "If I had known he was that kind of a fellow, hang me if I would have wasted either good liquor or good coffee on him."

"He can't have got very far off, if you say he was here only a few minutes ago," Blakely observed.

"It isn't ten minits since I gave him the coffee," the woman declared. stoutly.

"I'll go in search of him immediately; I will surely be able to overtake him, having the advantage of being on horseback. There's only two ways in which he can go toward Sandy Hook or to Long Beach."

"Yes, he can't go anywhere else, for thar's the ocean on one side and Shrewsbury River on the other. Cuss me! if

I wouldn't like to have a leetle talk with him myself, jest for to tell him what I think of his meanness!" the veteran grumbled.

Blakely hastened down-stairs into the open air, closely followed by the annoyed couple, anxious to know what had become of their guest.

There was an old fellow mending nets a short distance away, and from where he sat he commanded a view of the shed and window.

Blakely questioned him, but was unable to obtain any information, for the man protested that not a soul had he seen, although at last he admitted, under a close cross-examination, that he had been so busily engaged at his work that a man might have passed by without attracting his observation.

Just as Blakely succeeded in extorting this fact, the bell or a locomotive rung.

"Hallo! what train is that?" he asked.

"Up for York," was the answer.

"Has the man had time to get from the house to the depot so as to catch that train?"

There was a difference of opinion in regard to this. The woman thought he had, the fisherman said, decidedly, that he had not, and the old fellow shrewdly threw a little light on the matter by remarking: "It depends on how good the critter was on to his legs; mebbe he mought, and then ag'in he moughtn't."

Blakely thought the easiest way for him to ascertain the truth was to jump into the saddle and ride to the station, and this he lost no time in doing, first expressing his thanks to the honest couple for the interest they had taken in the search.

"But how 'bout this here boat?" the fisherman questioned as Blakely vaulted into the saddle. "Is it your'n?"

"Oh, that is all right; keep it for your trouble," the sailor replied, as he rode off. Blakely made the gift with a free conscience, for he felt perfectly sure that the abductor of the girl would never dare to return to claim the property.

In a few minutes he reached the depot. The depot master was the only one around, and he was an old man, and rather inclined to be stupid, and decidedly crusty in his manner.

"He hadn't seen any strange, dark complexioned man — had a good deal too much to do to bother his bead 'bout who got on the trains, or who got off," and that was all the satisfaction that the sailor was able to get from him.

Blakely rode back again toward the beach; he was convinced that his surmise was correct. He had got on the track of the man, and the fellow, catching sight of him, got out of the window and escaped by the train, and then a bright idea flashed into his head. He would ride to the telegraph office at Long Branch and send a dispatch to Mr. Anchona, telling him to be at the dock in New York with the necessary officers, and arrest the abductor when he arrived on the boat which connected with the train at Sandy Hook. The boat took over an hour to run up from the Hook to the city, and if the old gentleman acted promptly, the rascal might be trapped, thanks to the tongue of the lightning, even at the very moment that he was congratulating himself that he had given his pursuer the slip.

The operator promised to put the message right through when the necessity of haste was explained.

After this operation was performed, Blakely turned his attention again to the beach. The man had come ashore, clinging to the overturned boat, but no clew had he gained in regard to the girl. If she had met a watery grave when the craft capsized, then her body ought to have come ashore somewhere in the same neighborhood.

And as Blakely rode along, puzzling his wits over the matter, the remembrance of the broken mast of the boat occurred to him.

"And the sail, too!" he cried; "what became of the mast and sail? Evidently the breaking of the mast capsized the boat; both of the passengers were thrown into the sea, the man managed to get on the boat and so keep from sinking; why then may it not be possible that the girl clung to the mast and sail?

"Decidedly then my game now is to find out if any such thing has come ashore anywhere along the coast," be exclaimed.

In pursuance of this plan he rode back to Galilee and recommenced his inquiries, this time seeking for a broken mast with a sail attached.

With the perseverance of a bloodhound he hunted for a clew, and at last, by a group of shanties, just at the edge of Atlanticville, he found what he sought.

"A mast and sail?" repeated the old, weather-beaten fellow who was mending a boat on the beach, "Ay, ay, messmate, I think I see'd a strange mast and sail this morning, a-spread out to dry by old Jimmy White's shanty. He lives over yander, on the Shrewsbury, and when I see'd it, I reckoned he had helped to it, the old pirate! Don't you b'lieve a word he says, mister, for he'll lie out of it, if he kin, the blasted old shark!"

Thanking the man for his information, Blakely went at once in search of the house of the "old pirate," as the fisherman termed the person upon whose premises he had seen the broken mast and sail.

Blakely had no difficulty in finding the spot, for everybody seemed to be well acquainted with Jim White, and what was singular, no one had a good word for him; nearly all of whom Blakely inquired the direction went out of their way to take a fling at the old man, so that Blakely naturally came to the conclusion that White must be a pretty hard case.

The house — which was nothing more than a two-story shanty, built out of rough boards — occupied by this man of unsavory reputation stood all alone on a little point jutting out into the river.

A grizzled old sea-dog, whom Blakely immediately guessed to be White, sat upon the end of an overturned boat, smoking a short clay pipe which appeared to be as ancient as its owner.

The old man surveyed the rider with the utmost unconcern as he came up, never taking the trouble to remove the pipe from his mouth.

Upon the grass by the side of the house, spread out apparently to dry, was a broken mast with a sail attached.

Blakely's heart beat quickly as he recognized the objects, for there wasn't any doubt in his mind that it was the mast and sail which had belonged to the boat.

"How are you?" said the sailor, as he pulled in his steed and halted at the edge of the place.

"Howdy?" grunted the old man.

"Had quite a storm last night?"

"Dunno," responded the other.

White possessed keen eyes, despite his years, and had noticed the glance of satisfaction which had appeared upon the rider's face when he caught sight of the mast and sail.

"I am in search of a boat which was blown 'round Sandy Hook in the gale last night."

"W'ot do you come here for? Why don't you go over yonder to the beach? You ain't green enough, are ye, to think a boat could travel over the land into this here water, no matter how big the blow?"

"Oh, that is all right; I know where the boat is."

"Oh, you do?"

"Yes, she lies up at Galilee."

"W'ot are you a-wasting yer time a-chinning round here 'bout yer boat if you know wbar she is? Why don't you go and git her and not waste time?"

"The boat had a mast and sail in her when she came round the Hook last night, but when she came ashore this morning she was floating keel upward with only the stump of the mast left; the mast itself and the sail were gone."

"Ay, ay, that's the way things allers go in a blow."

"That's the mast and sail yonder."

"You lie, you son of a sea cook!" cried the old man, laying his pipe down and rising to his feet in a sudden fit of rage. "Don't you dare to come here and say I know anything 'bout yer blamed old mast and sail! How do I know that you ever had such a thing? and as for that 'ere rag and bit of timber, why, I've owned it for a year!"

Blakely understood at once the kind of a man that he had run across, and he had been an officer aboard too long not to know how to take care of such a customer.

The sailor was a man weighing a hundred and fifty pounds, tough as a pine-knot, and knew how to "handle himself" as well as any bully that ever played cock of the walk in the forecastle.

Without a word he dismounted from his horse, walked quietly up to the abusive White, and before that worthy comprehended what the stranger was up to, had him by the throat and shook him, as a terrier shakes a rat, until his teeth fairly chattered.

"I'm a liar, am I?" Blakely observed, and then he gave the old ruffian another shake, "and you've had that almost new canvas a year, you scoundrel?" and he tightened his grip on the other's throat until White's knee bent under him.

"Gug-gug-gug!" gasped the old wrecker, almost strangled.

Then, satisfied that he had taken some of the insolence out of him, Blakely let go his hold and the old fellow stumbled back and fell in a sitting posture on the boat.

His face for a moment was a study — fear and rage were strangely blended. As soon as he could get his breath he gasped:

"W'ot in blazes do you mean a-coming here and a-treating me in this here way? I'll have the law on you, see if I don't! Do you s'pose you kin come here and choke me like a blamed hen and think that I am a-going to stand it? Not much, if I know myself — not if my name is Jim White. I'll make you sweat for choking me afore you're a day older, and don't you forget it, neither!"

"You mustn't be so free with that ugly tongue of yours. I do not allow any man to call me a liar with impunity," the sailor answered. "I know this mast and sail have not been in your possession four-and-twenty hours, and I can easily bring witnesses to prove it, too!"

"Blast that measly John Riley and his son!" old White muttered. "I see'd the two a-spying round here this morning. Darn my skin, if I don't git even with them for it! Why don't they ketch their crabs and mind their own business?"

Blakely guessed that one of the parties to whom White referred was the man who had put him on the scent.

"But as far as the mast or sail is concerned I don't want either of them," Blakely remarked, "I am in search of information concerning the girl who came ashore at the same time as the mast and sail."

The old man assumed an air of ignorance, but the sailor fancied he detected a slight twinkle in his eyes.

"A gal?"

"Yes, a young girl who was in the boat when it was blown around Sandy Hook, and who, when the boat upset, saved herself by clinging to the mast and so was borne ashore."

"Waal, nobody see'd no young gal spread out here to dry, did they?" old White asked, assuming a humorous tone.

"Where is she — you rescued her, I suppose?" asked the sailor, coming at once to the point.

"W'ot do you ax sich a question for?" responded the old man, sulkily. "You know all 'bout it, in course. The sail and mast is yourn, and I pulled the gal outer the water, and mebbe killed her afterwards. It's a wonder you don't bring that up ag'in me, you're so mighty smart!"

"Oh, I do not pretend to know everything, my friend, but as the body of the girl has come ashore, it is reasonable to suppose that she did not perish when the boat capsized, and as I had an idea that she might have been saved by using the mast and sail as a support, when I find those articles in your possession, I assume that it is not impossible you may know something of the girl."

"Waal, mister, I'll own up to them things; I found 'em on the beach, but that wasn't no gal with them."

Blakely would have been apt to believe that he was on a wrong scent had there not been something about the old man's manner which made him suspect he was not telling all he knew about the matter.

"But you found her, though, for all that?" he replied, fixing his eyes sternly on the old rascal's face.

"Oh, yes, of course I did! and I've got her here, hid right under this 'ere boat," and he rapped the wood with his hand, then he laughed hoarsely. "Say! you 'pear to be mighty anxious 'bout this here gall. Don't you want to hire me to look for her?"

Blakely drew a long breath; the secret of the old man's stubborn denial was revealed. He wanted to make some money out of the matter.

"You shall be paid for your trouble, of course."

"Now you're talking. How much?"

"Well, any reasonable sum."

"Wot do you call a reasonable sum? That's the point on which thar may be a big difference of opinion," observed the old man, with a grin.

"Oh, I will leave that to you."

"How does a thousand dollars strike you?"

"A thousand dollars!" cried Blakely in amazement at the outrageous demand.

"That is wot I said; a thousand dollars; and I reckon from wot you say 'bout the gal she would be cheap at double the money."

Now, as Blakely hadn't said a word about the girl's looks or qualifications, these words convinced him that the old man did know something of her, but of course such a sum as a thousand dollars was out of the question.

"You are crazy, old man! If you were to say five or ten dollars I might employ you to search for her!"

"Bah! what is five or ten dollars to a gentleman like me?" he exclaimed. "It will take a thousand to make it worth my while."

"Oh, we can't trade, so search for her myself."

Blakely retraced his steps to where his horse stood, and mounted him.

"Try all you like, and if you can't find her, then call on me with the money, and I'll see what I kin do."

"Oh, you're an old rascal, and I don't believe a word you say!" Blakely cried, as he galloped off.

This was merely done to throw the wrecker off his guard, for Blakely was convinced that the man did know something of the girl. What he wanted now was time to summon the banker from New York.

Again the electric wires were brought into play, and a full account telegraphed to Mr. Anchona.

The chase was getting interesting, for the sailor believed the end was near.

CHAPTER XX.

STRAIGHT for Brand's heart was the blow aimed, and the stroke was given with all the power that dwelt in the assassin's frame.

It seemed as if a miracle alone could save the life of the human sleuth-hound.

But Brand was one of those men who, by means of brain and courage, work miracles.

The glittering, bodkin-like dagger, sharp as a razor, penetrated the cloth of the coat, and then, encountering a solid substance beneath, snapped in twain, close to the handle.

With a shrill cry of alarm the assassin recoiled, for she realized immediately that a surprise was in store for her.

Brand smiled; he had suddenly recovered the use of his muscles, and the sleepy, stolid look which his face had worn disappeared as if by magic.

"Oh, you devil! you have tricked me!" she cried, in bitter anger.

"I was Brace's comrade, but I do not think I am destined to share Brace's fate," Brand remarked, speaking in the most matter-of-fact way, and just as if nothing uncommon had occurred.

"What manner of man are you? And by what miracle have you escaped?"

The woman had wrought herself up to a fearful pitch of excitement; her face was distorted with passion, and she trembled in every limb.

"Oh, I'm the ordinary kind of man — haven't any more brains than the law allows, or else I never should have tumbled into this trap so stupidly. I had an idea you would try the same game on me that had been successful with poor Brace, but you see that is where I wronged you; I didn't give you credit for being as smart as you are. I own up! You fooled me most beautifully this time. I hadn't the least suspicion that there was anything crooked about the matter, and I walked into the snare with my eyes open, never dreaming of danger; but the moment I swallowed the wine I knew what was up, although when the stuff is administered in that way there is hardly any perceptible taste of it. It was an old acquaintance, and I recognized it. It must have been a pretty good sized dose, judging from the speedy manner in which it forced my esteemed friend here," and he glanced at the hotel clerk, who lay back in the easy-chair as senseless as a log. "But I am an old opium-eater. Years ago, when trouble nearly drove me crazy, I found relief in that lethe-producing drug, and become so used to it that I could take, without harm, a quantity large enough to almost kill a dozen men; but before I became an absolute slave a tide of fortune set in, and little by little I have weaned myself from its use; and now you will understand why the dose failed. I saw I was in a trap and I was determined to turn the tables on you and I flatter myself that I have performed that little job in a superior manner. Believing me to be helpless in your power, you threw off the mask, and during this short interview I learned more about you than I could have found out by myself in a month, even if I had had great good luck."

"Oh, you are a very devil!" the woman hissed, fiercely, and she brandished the useless weapon in the air, as though meditating another stroke.

"You cannot deceive me — you wear a breast-plate!"

And this was the truth. During one of his European trips Brand had purchased a shirt of mait made of the once famous Milan steel; it consisted of a series of rings curiously linked together, and was proof against the point of any knife that was ever forged, and in fact the pistol-ball that would make an impression upon it would have to be discharged from a superior weapon.

"Oh, no, I have been dipped in the famous spring which made all the old-time heroes invulnerable to either steel or lead," Brand answered, rising, and at the same time producing a pair of handcuffs from his pocket.

"Come," he said, "hold out your wrists so I can snap on the bracelets. You have played a bold game — played it deuced well, but the end has come."

The woman burst into a hollow laugh, and never in all his experience did Brand listen to merriment more strained or unnatural.

"Upon my word, Brand, you are a terrible fellow!" she exclaimed. "If I had had any idea of what kind of a man you really are, I should have thought twice before I attempted to entrap you. Of course I knew you by reputation well enough; I knew that you had made some marvelous captures and that of all the man-hunters in the country the bold souls under the ban of the law dreaded you far more than any of the rest, but although I guessed you were far superior to your fellows, yet, as I flattered myself that I had more brains than all the detectives put together, I did not feel any doubt in regard to the result when I determined to measure strength with you. Brace was supposed to be a very great detective, and the knowledge that he had been put upon the trail was always enough to make the boldest criminal take heed, but skillful as he was, I entrapped and slew him without the least trouble."

"Let me warn you," Brand hastened to say at this point, "to be careful how you speak, for as an officer of justice I am bound to tell you, as an honest man, that any disclosures you may make to me will surely be used against you."

"Oh, what do I care!" exclaimed the woman, apparently reckless. "I have played a bold game, and for a time laughed to scorn all the efforts of the authorities to entrap me; and now when my time has come, why should I not die as game as I have lived? You yourself must acknowledge that I have made a good fight. You did not succeed in entrapping me by the use of your wits, but solely by accident. With all your skill and cunning you walked into the trap as blindly as though you were a green country boy, instead of a man who bears the reputation of being the greatest detective that the country has ever known. Naught but accident, I repeat, enabled you to escape — an accident which was impossible for the keenest wits to foresee or provide against. I am only mortal. I am not possessed of supernatural knowledge; how was it possible for me to guess you were an opium-eater, and so able to take with impunity the drug which rendered your companion as helpless as a dead man? Bah! I can read the signs which predict the future as well as any one who breathes the breath of life! The fatal event shows me that my career is ended. Why, then, should I attempt to struggle against fate? It is useless! Man I can fight and conquer, but when fate steps into the list it is as well to yield at first, as to be bruised and wounded by an unavailing struggle."

This speech confirmed Brand in the impression which he had formed when the particulars of the mysterious murder first became known to him; the secret assassin was a little touched in the upper story. But he was glad to find she was disposed to take the matter coolly, for he hated to have trouble with a woman, even though she was no better than a female fury.

"Well, it's the fortune of war, I suppose; so, if you permit me to snap these little ornaments upon your wrists, we'll be going," he remarked.

"But why is it necessary to put on those horrid things?" she exclaimed; "I will go with you quietly enough; I will not attempt to resist; you see, I am perfectly passive — I am resigned to my fate; destiny itself fights against me; I realize the fact and know that it will be useless for me to struggle."

Brand shook his head. He had been tricked in this fashion once before. A woman had begged to be spared the humiliation of going through the public streets with the handcuffs on her delicate wrists; he had consented, and the moment he was out of the house the prisoner's confederates assaulted him, and so enabled her to escape. If she had had the bracelets on the trick would not have been accomplished so easily.

"You will not?"

"No, madam, I regret that I cannot oblige you; for it is my rule to always put the bracelets on a prisoner."

"Oh, well, I suppose I must submit, then, as I cannot help myself; but it is a shameful degradation." She extended her writits. Brand, deceived by the apparent submission, bent forward to adjust the handcuffs, when, with lightning-like quickness, the woman dealt him a terrible blow between his eyes that staggered him back; falling against a chair he lost his balance and came to the ground. This gave the prisoner a chance to dart through the door into the adjoining room. In a twinkling Brand was on his feet and threw himself against the door.

CHAPTER XXI.

BRAND was a brainy fellow; it was not often he met his match, but in this case the woman certainly had duped him.

After passing through the door she had both locked and bolted it upon the other side, and when the detective flung himself against it he could not stir it, being a solid affair, put together in a workmanlike manner, and not to be easily forced.

"The infernal vixen!" cried Brand, greatly enraged, smarting under his defeat and the effects of the blow, which had been delivered with all the precision of a professional pugilist.

The detective had guessed the woman's game. From the other room, which was a bed-chamber, a door probably gave access to the entry, and while he was engaged in forcing an entrance into the apartment, she would be able to make her escape.

Brand hesitated for a moment. Which door could he break open the easiest? That was the question he asked himself, and almost immediately decided that as the main door opened into the room, while the one he was at swung exactly the contrary, he would do better to keep on in his attack.

Drawing back a few paces he planted a powerful kick on the door, right beside the lock, which had never been made with the idea of resisting such an attack, and so the attachments gave way at once and the door flew open.

Only a minute or two had elapsed since the woman entered the room, but it was evident she had made good use of her time, for when Brand rushed into the apartment the culprit had disappeared.

As he expected, a door led from the bed-chamber into the hall, and an examination disclosed that it was locked and the key missing.

The woman had evidently passed out of the door into the entry, and by the device of locking the door after her, had most effectually put a stop to pursuit.

Brand's resolution was soon taken. He had a stout knife in his pocket and he thought he could succeed in forcing back the bolt, as the lock was so arranged as to afford him an opportunity of working at it.

This operation was accomplished with very little trouble, and the detective found himself at liberty again.

That the woman would lose no time in getting out of the hotel he did not doubt.

She was attired in a plain dark dress, and as he had not noticed her hat or cloak in the inner apartment, he presumed she had caught them up in her flight, so she was fully equipped for the street, and would not attract attention by an unusual costume.

Straight then, to the "ladies' entrance" of the hotel went Brand, and there inquired of the colored man, who had charge of the door, if he had seen a lady go out, describing "Miss Madriea."

"Yas, sah," responded the hotel Cerberus, "bout five minutes ago. You mean dat foreign lady wid de big diamonds?"

"Yes; did she seem to be in a hurry?"

"No, sah, I didn't notice anything out of de common."

Brand thanked the man for the information, slipped a quarter into his hand and went out into the street, hoping that he would be able from some one of the loungers, usually to be found around the outside of the hotel, to discover which way the fugitive had gone.

He secured a clew from the very first man whom he accosted, one of the hackmen whose coach stood by the edge of the pavement.

"A lady in black? Oh, yes, sir, she took Jack Mulligan's coach to the Twenty-third Street Ferry; she wanted to catch a train on the Erie Road for Buffalo."

In order to be sure that there wasn't any mistake about the matter, Brand got the man to give him as good a description as he could of the lady, for it didn't seem possible that she would be so foolish as to "give away" the route that she had taken.

The description tallied exactly with his bird, and when the detective reflected upon the matter he saw the game that the fugitive had made up her mind to play.

From the hotel, by means of a carriage, the Twenty-third Street Ferry -the up-town depot of the Erie Railway — could be easily reached in ten minutes. She calculated that she would have at least ten minutes' start of her pursuer; she could gain the ferry by the time that the trail was taken up — and if she made this conjecture it was correct, for Brand had been detained fully ten minutes. To put the police machinery in motion to intercept her would take fifteen or twenty minutes more, and by that time she would be able to get out of the way, for that she had any idea of leaving the city the detective did not for an instant believe; but at the same time it wouldn't do any harm to send out a general alarm, requesting the police to detain Miss Marita Madriea. So Brand hurried to the telegraph station and sent a dispatch to the central office, then returned to wait the coming of the driver.

Not long was he kept in suspense. In about ten minutes a hack drove up, and the driver looked exactly like a man who would answer to such a name as Jack Mulligan.

Brand accosted him and found that his guess was correct.

The man had driven the lady in black to the Erie depot, at the foot of Twenty-third Street, but whether she had entered the depot or not, was more than he could say, as after he had been paid he drove immediately back to the hotel in order to keep an appointment with another customer, and so had not noticed where his fare had gone.

The detective thanked the man for the information and turned away.

"The game is up for the present," he muttered. "The whole thing was a plant to throw me off the track. She has not gone out of the city, but would have been wise if she had done so, for, by Heaven! I'll have her, no matter how skillfully she may hide herself. New York is a big place to play at hide-and-seek, but that doesn't make any difference, for in the end a fugitive can be hunted down as well here as in the smallest village; it only takes a little more time — that is all."

Brand was considerably nettled by the result of this affair. In all his professional experience he had never been so skillfully beaten; but the fact only made him more determined to turn the tables upon this cunning adversary, for he felt that she was a foeman worthy of his steel.

Re-entering the hotel, he took the superintendent to one side and explained to him all that had occurred.

The astonishment of that gentleman was great.

"Upon my word I never was so completely tricked in my life," he declared. "I'm an old hand at the business, and I thought I could detect an impostor without much trouble;

but I must own up beat in this case, for I had not the slightest suspicion that there was anything crooked about the woman."

Then the two hastened up-stairs in hopes to secure a clew.

The clerk was still in the easy-chair, insensible to all surroundings.

"That dose was a strong one, and it will be eight or ten hours before he recovers from the effects of it," Brand remarked.

"Is there any danger of serious results?"

"Oh, no nothing more than a dull headache, just as if he had been on a prolonged spree, that's all."

Then, at Brand's suggestion, the clerk was placed upon the bed, so that he might be comfortable during his enforced sleep.

A large Saratoga trunk stood in a corner of the room.

"How could a man suspect that the party wasn't solid, coming with a trunk like that, worth twenty-five or thirty dollars?" exclaimed the superintendent, with a grimace.

The trunk was locked, and when Brand tested its weight he remarked how heavy it seemed.

"Oh, yes, that's the old game; when we come to open it we'll find that it is full of brickbats and such rubbish," the hotel man observed, dolefully. "The trick hasn't been played for so long that I had really begun to believe it had died out."

The superintendent had a bunch of small keys, and just by chance one of them happened to fit the lock, so they were able to open the trunk without violence.

The hotel official was correct in his guess; the trunk was filled to the brim with bricks carefully wrapped in rags and paper.

"Hang me if I understand it, though!" the superintendent exclaimed, "She has only been here a few days, and the trunk is worth about enough to cover her bill."

"Her game was not to swindle your hotel, but to get me into a trap so as to be able to put me out of the way," Brand remarked; "but after the tight squeeze she had this time, I reckon she won't be apt to try the game again."

Being now satisfied that no further information could be gained in the hotel, the detective posted to the railway depot at the foot of Twenty-third Street, and there made diligent inquiries in regard to the woman in black, but not the slightest bit of intelligence could he gain.

Both the ticket-seller and the gate-keeper, who had been on duty since six o'clock, were perfectly sure that no such woman had been seen by them.

"It is as I expected," muttered Brand, as he turned away; "nothing but a plant to throw me off the scent if I was in hot pursuit. Well, the first trick is hers, but one trick don't make a game; and as she knows me in my own proper person, it is now in order for me to get down to real work. Carlton Brand must vanish for awhile, and in his place a second detective must rise, more potent than the first!"

CHAPTER XXII.

AND now we must return to the girl upon whom fortune had frowned so perversely ever since her arrival in the New World.

From the time when she had fallen in a swoon on the beach, exhausted by the terrible struggle with the waves, until she woke to consciousness in what was apparently the cellar of a house, all was a blank. When she recovered her senses she found herself lying upon a little bed, with an old man and woman bending over her.

A small lamp, placed upon one of the stairs that led to a trap-door, dimly illuminated the scene.

The old woman had bathed her face with camphor water, and under the simple treatment consciousness soon returned.

Helena looked around in amazement at the dingy apartment, the ceiling so near that a tall man could not have stood upright, the earth walls, the utter absence of windows, as well as the uncouth appearance of the old couple excited her wonder, and she could not possibly imagine what had become of her.

The fisherman and his wife, watching her with the eyes of hawks, noted the opening of her brilliant orbs, and comprehended that reason had once again resumed its sway.

"Do you feel better, deary?" croaked the old woman, endeavoring to soften her hard features into a sympathetic glance.

"Where am I?" was the natural question of Helena, as soon as she recovered strength enough to speak.

"Oh, you're all right, ducky! don't you be afeared!" replied the old man.

"But an awful tight squeeze you've had of it, you poor thing," the woman remarked. "I tell you what it is, my dear, it was a lucky thing for you that my old man and me happened to be a-passing along the beach and see'd you a-lying there, as cold and as stiff, jest for all the world like you was dead; but we fetched you along with us, and I reckon now that you've got yer eyes open, and kin use your tongue a leetle, that you'll cling to life for a while longer, anyhow."

"But you mustn't fatigue yourself by talking much, or else the doctor says you'll be apt to slip your cable and slide into the other world, for sure," observed the old man.

"The doctor! has there been a doctor to see me?" Helena asked, astonished.

"Oh, yes, I reckon he's been here three or four times — hain't he, old woman?" White replied, with a wink to his wife.

She was quick to understand his meaning.

"Yes, yes, and if it a-hadn't been for the stuff he forced down your throat, you would never have come to life again."

"Why, how long have I been here?" she asked, amazed, for she was not conscious that there had been any great lapse of time since the moment when she fell fainting upon the beach.

"Lemme see! is it three or four days, old woman?"

"Four," responded the hag, speaking in such an honest way that Helena did not for an instant doubt the assertion.

"Four days," she murmured, "and it does not seem to me as if it had been more than four hours."

The wrecker chuckled in his sleeve, for he saw that the girl was completely deceived.

"Waal, you see that is because you have bin out of yer head, a-raying away here like all possessed. Fact! I never thought that you would come out of your crazy fit, but the doctor said you would, and it 'pears he was right."

"And, sakes alive! child, you've no idea how glad me and my old man was when we see'd you were a-coming to. Why, it was only yesterday that I sed to my old man, sed I, 'Lands! if that gal dies here onto our hands, won't it be a downright shame!" declared the woman, lying with an ease and art that really excited the admiration of her confederate.

"Oh, I am not going to die, for I feel quite well. I am weak, that is all, but I am getting stronger every moment, and I think I can get up!"

"Oh, lands, no!" screamed the old hag. "The doctor said as how you wasn't to be moved for a week!"

"Yes, he said it would be your death if you attempted to get up!" the man added.

Helena was amazed, for now that the faintness had passed away she felt about as well as usual, and not at all like one who had been confined to a sick-bed for the better part of a week.

"I think the doctor must be wrong, for I do not feel at all unwell, and I am sure I feel quite strong enough to get up."

"Better mind what the doctor says; he knows, and since you have been saved from an awful death, you ought not to fly in the face of Providence be trying to do what you hadn't oughter," the wrecker's wife remarked.

"Yes, and 'ticularly when there isn't any need of it!" declared the old man. "Now, that you kin talk, you kin tell me about your friends, and I will send word so as to let 'em know where you are."

"Yes, deary, and you can stay here, nice and comfortable, until they come for you," added the old woman, with a leer.

The game that this well-mated pair decided upon playing, when they discovered the girl lying helpless upon the beach, was an extremely simple one. From her lady-like appearance, they thought she must be a member of the upper-ten, and they concluded by getting her into their clutches they would be able to get a good sum of money from her folks as a reward for their "kindness," and it was their intention to hold on to the girl until a "stake" was forthcoming.

Now Helena, although nothing but a child, and one who had mingled but little with the great world, yet being well educated, was no simpleton, and then, too, she was gifted with an unusual amount of common sense, besides possessing the peculiar instinct so common to womankind.

The impression produced upon her by these people into whose hands she had fallen was not favorable.

She distrusted them; their evil faces impressed her most unfavorably, and so she briefly said she would not comply with their request. She had no friends to whom she could send; she was all alone in the world, and had no one but herself to depend upon. She did not deem it necessary to relate the whole of her story. She knew that she was to be met by some one upon arriving at New York, and that was all.

She further said that she did not wish to trespass upon their kindness, but would go to the city as soon as she was well enough, and she felt sure that it would not take long for her to recover her strength.

"Well, you'll have to stay for a couple of days anyway." the old man replied, with an ill grace, "for the doctor is away and will not return until then, and he sed if we let you go, your death would be at our door; and it's by his orders, too, that we fixed up this place for you, for he sed you must be kept where the daylight couldn't get at you, 'cos it would be apt to throw you into a brain fever."

"It is very strange," the girl murmured, perplexed, for her instinct told her that there was something wrong about the matter. "I know I am strong enough to get up, and I feel sure 1 can take care of myself. I haven't a great deal of money, but enough to pay for your trouble, so, if you please, I'll get up and go away."

The old couple shook their heads in decided disapprobation.

"Oh, we couldn't think of letting you go till the doctor comes, 'cos if anything was to happen to you folks would blame us, and maybe the officers would put us in jail," the wrecker exclaimed.

Helena was not in the least deceived by these specious words.

She understood that she was a prisoner, and would not be allowed to depart, though why she was detained, and how long her captivity would last, she could not guess.

With a shrewdness that few would have believed could have dwelt in so innocent a maiden, she did not make any further objections, but appeared resigned to her fate. The fisherman and his wife were completely deceived and after a little more conversation retired, advising the girl to get all the sleep that she possibly could, saying that they would not disturb her until she called for them by knocking on the ceiling.

"When you get hungry and feel like a good cup of tea, just pound away and I'll fotch it to ye," was the parting injunction of the old woman.

They did not remove the lamp, for they were so completely deceived by the girl that they did not dream that any idea of flight was in her mind.

But with the return of her reason came the firm determination to escape from her prison-house as soon as possible.

When she attempted to get up, though, she found that she was still quite weak; she had miscalculated her strength, so she lay down again.

And then, after an hour or so, she began to feel sleepy, and, closing her eyes, was soon wrapped in a strength-giving slumber.

She slept until the day was well advanced, and when she awoke she felt undeniably hungry.

Summoning the old woman, she said she would be glad to have a cup of tea.

Mrs. White hastened to prepare a simple meal, and after Helena had eaten it, she felt like another girl.

She was careful, though, not to allow this fact to become known, for she did not wish her jailers to take any extra precautions so as to make it more difficult for her to escape.

So, after eating, she lay down again upon the bed, and the old hag departed, perfectly satisfied that the girl was disposed to be contented.

CHAPTER XXIII.

AFTER sending the dispatch, Blakely sat down in the waiting-room of the depot. Nothing more could be done until he heard from New York.

He was convinced he was on the right track.

The old scamp had possession of the sail and mast, and from the way in which he had spoken of the girl it was clear that he knew what she was like.

Blakely thought he could guess the man's scheme. The unfortunate maiden had come ashore in an almost insensible state, and White, happening to be prowling along the beach, had come across her. Thinking a reward might be offered for her discovery, he had conveyed her to some secure place, and was determined not to reveal where she was until he was well paid for his trouble.

Blakely had calculated that it would take about two hours for his message to reach New York and an answer to come; and so, when the end of the time approached, he sauntered out on the platform to be in readiness for the dispatch.

He was at the main Long Branch depot where the "all rail" route from the city comes in, and as he reached the platform a train from New York drew up to the station.

To Blakely's astonishment, Mr. Anchona, accompanied by the old lawyer and a couple of rough-looking men, got out.

"I received both your dispatches, all right," he said, "but the infernal telegraph company delayed the first message so that we were too late to intercept the boat. I hurried immediately to the main office of the Western Union to wire you, and there received your second dispatch, and, luckily, we just had time to catch a train, so here we are, ready for business. These two gentlemen represent the law," and the old banker smiled while the two, who looked more like prize-fighters than officers of the law, grinned and winked in a highly significant manner.

"From your dispatch, brief as it was, I gathered that the party we have to deal with is inclined to be ugly," continued the banker, "and in all such cases I have always found it was good policy to advance in such force as to preclude resistance from being offered. If we went alone the fellow might laugh at us, but with these gentlemen to back our cause, I've no doubt when our man discovers how matters stand he will be inclined to listen to reason."

And Blakely, when he took a good look at the muscular and determined-appearing fellows, came to the same conclusion.

"We had better get ahead as soon as possible," the lawyer suggested, "as we have no time to lose if we mean to conclude the business before dark."

Blakely explained that a carriage must be procured, and this was soon done.

The four gentlemen got in, the young sailor mounted his horse, put himself in the advance, and off they went.

Before starting the lawyer was careful to whisper in Blakely's ear:

"Stop the carriage far enough from the house so that the driver will not be able to either overhear or see what occurs. We may have to proceed a little irregularly in this matter, and we do not want any witness to make trouble afterward."

Blakely understood the necessity that there was for this, and so halted the coach when they arrived at a point about a quarter of a mile from the house of the old wrecker.

The coachman did not regard the invasion with any particular curiosity, for he took the party to be on a real-estate excursion, looking for a site of a new summer hotel, or something of that sort.

But old White was not in the least bit deceived. The moment he saw the "army" advancing over the sandy track of open country, and recognized Blakely in advance, he anticipated trouble.

He was occupying his usual seat upon the boat, and had got well into the enjoyment of a fresh pipe when he made the discovery.

"Old woman, old woman!" he yelled, "here's that pesky young cuss back, and he's got a big crowd with him. Jest bolt and bar the doors, for I'll bet they mean mischief; if they were a-coming to do the fair thing by me they wouldn't bring such a gang as that 'ere along!"

White and his dame had had a conference after Blakely's departure, so the woman understood exactly how matters stood.

While she made the fortress secure, the old man retained his seat, quietly puffing away at his pipe.

Anchona had a brief and authoritative way with him, like the majority of men who have become possessed of a great deal of money, and understand how much money can accomplish.

He walked straight up to the wrecker and looked him squarely in the eye, thereby causing White to scowl in an extremely ugly way.

"There's the mast and sail — now where is the girl?" he exclaimed, sternly.

"W'ot gal?" growled the other.

"Come, come, no nonsense, my man!" exclaimed Anchona, in a tone like a master addressing his slave. "You know what girl I mean, and where she is, well enough."

"Oh, do I?" replied the old fellow, rather awed by the manner of the other; "p'rhaps you know better 'bout the thing than I do myself?"

"The presence of that mast and sail on your premises is ample proof that you possess a knowledge of the matter, and I give you fair warning that I am not in a humor to stand any nonsense, and therefore the quicker you tell all you know, the better it will be for you."

"Did this young feller tell you w'ot I sed?" asked White, nodding his head toward Blakely.

"In regard to the thousand dollars that you demanded?"

"That's it — that's the p'int!"

"You are crazy, man! If you had said a dollar, now, for your trouble -"

"Oh, what are you giving me?" cried the old man, in a tone of disgust. "A dollar! What kind of a man do you take me for, anyhow? A dollar! W'ot's a dollar to me? Why, it ain't enuff to pay for the rum for the boys."

"Well, I think you and your boys will have to do without rum if you depend upon getting any money from me to pay for it. Come! I'll give you just three minutes to answer my questions — where is the girl?" and the millionaire took out his watch and sprung open the case, while White surveyed him with a mysterious scowl.

"One!" counted Anchona.

"Ain't I going to have anything for my trouble?" growled the old man, hardly knowing what to make of these summary proceedings.

"Nothing at all, sir, excepting that if you are not careful how you conduct yourself you may secure lodgings in the nearest jail, too!"

"Jail! You be hanged!" White yelled, rising in a sudden fury. "I reckon that I ain't done nothing for to be put in jail for! You can't come here and skeer me to easy. Who are you, anyway? I don't know you-- I never saw you afore, and I reckon you don't own the hull state, for all you talk so big."

"The time is pretty nearly gone," cautioned Anchona.

"Oh, w'ot kin you do? You can't skeer me, nohow you kin fix it."

"Three!"

"Three be blowed! wot do I keer?"

"Arrest him!" the banker commanded.

The two men seized the fisherman with a quickness that took him by surprise, and before he could collect himself for a struggle a pair of handcuffs were snapped upon his wrists, and one of the men threatening him with a short club, which he produced from under his coat, warned him that if he attempted to "cut up rusty," he'd have a head put on him which he wouldn't get rid of for a month.

White fairly foamed at the mouth with rage. The old man had had several tussles with the local officials within the last few years, and as these worthies, being about as worthless as the usual run of village officials, had feared to enrage the so-called desperate man, he had always come out first best. But these strangers were evidently men of different metal and not to be frightened by words.

"Now, then, will you tell me where the girl is, or must we lug you off to jail and then break into your old shanty?" Anchona demanded.

"You don't dare! You ain't got no warrant!" the wrecker howled.

"Ain't we? well, now, old buffer! that is jest whar you are out, for we've got a hull pocket full!" cried one of the men.

"Governor, 'tain't any use to waste words upon such a cuss as this!" exclaims the other. "If he opens his head again I'll fetch him a lick that will shut him up for a week. Just say the word and we'll smash in the ranch as if it was an egg-shell!"

"Oh, you will, will you?" cried a shrill voice, and Mrs. White appeared at one of the upper windows with a double-barreled shot-gun. "Take off them handcuffs and get out of here, or I'll put a charge of buckshot inter your hides, you bloody-minded villains!" And she brandished the gun in a threatening manner to give due effect to her words.

But she had a terrible gang to deal with, as she speedily discovered, for no sooner had she finished her speech than, without a word of warning, both of the men drew revolvers from under their coats and opened fire on the window.

The moment she heard the bullets whistling through the air, followed by the dull thud as they entered the wood of the house, with a scream of horror she dropped the gun and fled.

Having thus routed the garrison, the men rushed up to the door and with a few vigorous kicks stove it in.

The fortress was captured.

CHAPTER XXIV.

WHEN old White witnessed the utter discomfiture of his better half, who on several occasions had "held the fort" successfully against half a dozen local officers, no one of whom dared to run the risk of getting a charge of buckshot in his precious body, he realized he had fallen into the hands of men who "meant business, every time," and immediately came to the conclusion that discretion was the better part of valor.

"Hol' on, hol' on!" he cried; "for goodness' sake, don't tear the hull house down! I'll gi'n in to once without making any more time 'bout it, but I think it's a cussed shame that you ain't willing to give me something for my trouble."

"Ah, it is rather late in the day to talk that way," Anchona remarked. "If you had commenced by being reasonable, I should have been willing to pay you a trifle if you have taken good care of the lady."

"I wouldn't have hurt her for the world!" the old rascal protested. "She was a leetle flighty — a leetle teched in the upper story, 'cos she had an awful night of it, and I didn't think it was right to let her go a-wandering 'bout, for fear she mought git inter bad hands, you know, who, p'rhaps, would hurt her, so I jest locked her up till I could find out 'bout her friends."

The face of the banker changed, and it was evident he was much agitated at the intelligence.

"Do I understand you to say that her mind is affected?" he asked.

"Yes, a leetle, but nothing to hurt, I reckon. You see, she had a terrible time. She came ashore, clinging to that mast and sail, and jest had strength to crawl up on the beach, then fainted dead away, and when I came along the tide was almost up to her. It was a flood tide and making in strong, you know, and if I had been twenty minutes later she would have been a goner, for the water would have got hold of her, and as she wouldn't have been able to fight ag'in' it, the surf would soon have battered the life out o' her."

"But she is safe now?" Anchona demanded, anxiously.

"Yes, a leetle weak and light-headed, but that is all. Why, the gal couldn't even tell me the name of her friends, although I offered for to send a message for to tell 'em where she was."

The banker understood the meaning of this; in bringing the girl across the ocean both he and his agents had been careful to keep in the background.

"Where is she? lead me to her at once. If I find your story to be correct, and you have taken good care of the girl, you shall not lose anything by it."

The face of the old man brightened when he found he was not going to be completely "left," to use the vernacular.

"Say, can't you have these leetle bracelets taken off?" White asked, holding out his manacled wrists; "I never did keer much for jewelry, anyhow."

"Take them off," commanded the banker to the men who held possession of the doorway, and who, having secured entrance, were waiting for orders.

One of them came up to the old man and removed the handcuffs.

"I'm ever so much obliged to ye," be remarked.

"And now produce the girl!" cried Anchona.

"All right; she's down into the cellar; I put her there 'cos she was a leetle restive and I didn't know but she would take it inter her head to run away."

The attacking party looked at the shanty inquisitively. Built on the level ground, there was not the slightest indication that there was any cellar under it.

The old man chuckled; he guessed the thoughts that were passing in his visitors' minds.

"Don't see much signs of a cellar,' do ye? I reckon that if I had chose to be ugly 'bout the matter, all on yees would have been a long time a-finding it out."

Then the old man led the way into the house, and as he entered, the woman, who had descended to the lower floor, met him with loud complaints.

"Did you see the devils shoot their pistols at me?" she cried. "It was a mercy that I wasn't killed. But I'll have the law on 'em, if there's any law in Jersey; see if I don't!"

"Oh, shet up, old woman, you made a good fight, but they were too much for you, that's all there is 'bout it. I don't bear no malice, though they did clap the bracelets onto me. They are going to do the right thing by us, when they see we didn't hurt the gal, but took as much keer on her as if she had been our own darter."

The woman was quick to alter her tone at this information.

"Well, I guess we did, the poor' dear child! Oh, good gentlemen, we have treated her exactly as if she had been our own flesh and blood, and she will tell you so when you see her, although she may complain because we didn't let her go; but, gracious! we didn't care to, 'cos she was all mixed up 'bout where she was going — couldn't tell 'bout her friends or nothing, and we was afeared that some harm might come to her. We put her down in the cellar, 'cos that was the only safe place in the house; she was as quiet as a lamb, gentlemen; we didn't have a bit of trouble with her. We told her that we'd send for her friends as soon as possible, and fixed up a bed so that she would be nice and comfortable. The cellar is dry, and although it's a leetle dark, it's a right place for anybody wot's a leetle sick."

"Don't waste any more time, but conduct us to the girl at once," Anchona exclaimed, impatiently.

"Certainly," responded White, pulling aside an old piece of oil-cloth that was laid upon the floor in front of the stove, and revealing a trap-door beneath; when this was lifted, a flight of steps leading down to the floor of the cellar was exhibited.

"The stairs are perfectly safe," observed the old man, as he descended into the underground apartment.

Anchona followed closely upon his heels. But hardly had they disappeared from view when a cry of alarm came from the old wrecker.

The cellar was empty — the girl gone.

The little cot-bed and chair, which had been placed in the apartment for the accommodation of the prisoner, were there all right, but the girl herself was not to be seen.

The cellar was only about ten feet square, being merely a hole scooped out in the earth, and about six feet deep. There was no way of lighting the place except by opening the trap-door.

White was not long in discovering how the girl had managed to escape.

As the old shanty was terribly out of repair, the gutters of the roof, instead of carrying the water away from the house as they ought to have done, discharged nearly all of it near one corner of the building, and, as a natural result, the water had made a hole through the earth into the cellar. The girl, upon discovering this fact, had found it an easy matter to tunnel through the loose earth until she made a passage large enough for her to creep out.

Anchona was terribly disappointed at this unexpected misfortune. At first the suspicion entered his mind that the old couple were deceiving him, and that the girl had not been with them at all, but their disgust and wrath upon discovering that the girl had been sharp enough to escape, were evidently genuine.

"I wouldn't have believed it if I hadn't seen it with my own eyes!" White declared, "Why; boss, when the old woman and me h'isted her down into the cellar she didn't seem to have as much life into her as a sick cat! Durn me, if it don't beat my time."

"She was a-playing 'possum!" declared the old woman, shrilly. "We war a couple of fools not to suspect that she war up to some mischief when she took the matter so quietly."

"We must go in search of her at once!" Anchona exclaimed, as he ascended from the underground apartment. "Can you form any idea how long it is since she escaped?"

The two shook their heads dubiously.

"Fact is" said the old man after a pause, "neither the misses nor me went near her arter 'bout eleven o'clock. 'Bout that time the old woman went down to see if she would take a bite of something, thinking she might be hungry. She said she would take a cup o' tea and some bread and butter, and the old woman fixed it for her: so she was there then; she was lying on the bed, a-pretending to be all used up, but now I reckon that it was all put on for to throw dirt in our eyes, and it did, too, blame her!"

"Where can she have gone? Ah, if the poor child had only waited; but then how could she know that friends would come so soon?" Anchona exclaimed, visibly affected.

"Gov'nor, she can't be very far off!" the old wrecker cried, thinking that he perceived a way to make some money out of the affair after all. "If all pitch right in we'll be sure to find her, or, anyway, if we don't find her, we can find out which way she went, for somebody must have seen her."

"No doubt about it, and we must lose no time, I'll give a hundred dollars to the man that finds the girl!" the New Yorker exclaimed.

"I'm in for the job!" White cried, with alacrity.

Five minutes later the party were upon the quest, Anchona, Blakely and the old lawyer going in one direction, the muscular New Yorker in another, and White setting off by himself.

But not the least bit of success attended any of their efforts, and up to eleven that night, when the search was reluctantly given up, not the slightest trace of the girl was obtained.

CHAPTER XXV.

RETURN we again to the cozy sanctum of Doc Lee. The clocks have just marked the hour of eleven, and the owner of the mansion, ensconced in a great easy-chair, was helping himself to brandy and soda from the bottles placed upon a small table drawn up to his side.

Lee, always colorless, was paler even than usual, and he seemed out of sorts. He tossed off the brandy — the best that money could buy — as though it was nothing but water, and it did not seem to produce any more effect upon him.

He had just come in, and had hardly got comfortably seated, when the servant whose business it was to attend to the front door came with the intelligence that Mr. May desired to speak to him.

"Show him up," commanded Lee.

In a few minutes May entered the room, being careful to close the door tightly behind him, and by this movement he gave Lee to understand that he had something of importance to communicate.

A serious look, too, rested Upon May's face, and any one with half an eye could see that he was materially disturbed.

"Take a chair, old fellow, and help yourself to the brandy," Lee said. "You must excuse my asking you to wait upon yourself, for I'm all tired out — played out expresses it exactly."

"That's all right," May rejoined, placing a chair by the side of the table, opposite to where the host sat, and helping himself to a liberal draught of the good liquor. "But what is the matter?" he asked, after draining the glass, "What have you been up to?"

"Oh, I fell in with a jolly party at the club this afternoon, and to pass the time away we indulged in a little draw-poker, and we became so interested in the game that we played from about three o'clock up to ten."

"Well, that was a long sitting."

"A deuced expensive one for me, too."

"How was that?"

"Hang me if I know! The very deuce seemed to be in the cards. If I held a good hand, some one else was sure to hold a better. Never in all my life did luck run more counter."

"Did you lose heavily?"

"Rather — ten or twelve thousand!" responded Lee, with a wry face, and then he sought consolation in another dose of brandy.

May whistled — his way of expressing vast astonishment.

"Well, well, you were put in a hole!"

"Yes, and between you and me, in strict confidence, I can't really afford to spare the money just now. It will make me deuced short. I've worked like a nigger; to pay like a prince; you can see for yourself that I am all used up."

"You certainly do not appear to be in first-class condition. Who were the parties?"

"Oh, I couldn't tell you that, Morgan, you know; the game was strictly on the quiet. We had one of the private card-rooms, and no one had the slightest suspicion that we were gambling on a great scale. But, to turn the conversation, what brings you over at this late hour? Something important, I presume."

"Yes, very important."

"So I imagined. Let me see! Why, I haven't seen you since the day we met on the steamer dock when the girl was expected."

"That's a fact; I've been busy, and then there wasn't anything of importance to communicate."

"Fire away!"

"Of course I have kept my eyes open, and thanks to the ingenious spy system that I devised, I can overhear every word that is said whenever Mr. Anchona has a conference with any one in his private office."

"That was a capital idea."

"Yes, and owing to it I have been as well informed how the search of the girl progresses as the banker himself."

"Well, has the search progressed at all — has any clew to the girl been discovered?"

"Yes, a clew has been found at last; not much of a one, but still, if followed up, it may amount to something. The girl was abducted from the deck of the steamer by a fellow in a boat, but why the outrage was done no one has the slightest idea. He was chased around Sandy Hook, then in a storm the boat upset, the girl floated to shore, clinging to the mast, was taken to the house of a fisherman, but fled from there just before Mr. Anchona arrived, and a diligent search has failed to discover where she went. That was two weeks ago. Anchona returned to New York, but left agents on the ground who kept up the search, and one of them to-day stumbled on the track, so immediately wired the banker. The girl, after leaving the house where she had been sheltered, went straight to a railway depot and took a train for New York."

"Aha!" cried Lee, who had been listening with the deepest attention. "she is in the city, then?"

"There doesn't seem to be any doubt of it."

"But how strange that it should have taken two weeks to make this discovery."

"It is easily explained. The station-agent from whom she bought her ticket and inquired the way to the city, went on a vacation immediately after the train departed, and did not return till yesterday. There does not seem to be any doubt about the matter, for the man describes the girl to a hair;

and then, too, he had a good reason for remembering her. When she came to pay for her ticket she had nothing but English money, and she explained that she had only been a few hours in the country. The agent was an accommodating fellow and took the money; he was coming to the city and he knew he could get it changed, so as to keep his accounts straight. This circumstance seems to fix the identity of the girl beyond a doubt."

"Yes, yes, certainly; the detective got upon the right track, but that was two weeks ago; what has become of the girl? How is it that if she is in the city no one has heard of her?"

"That is exactly what bothers Anchona and his assistants, who are Straub, his lawyer, and a Mr. Blakely, who was an officer on the steamer that brought the girl over, but who has left the service and taken a commission in Anchona's sanctum this evening. Blakely is the man who gained the information from the station-agent."

"He must be a persevering fellow to keep at it all this time," Lee observed.

"From the conversation I gathered that he is greatly interested in the girl. He is the man that commanded the boat that gave chase to the abductor."

"I see; a case of love at first sight, I presume," observed the other, with a sneer.

"Well, it looks a little like it, but he has given up beat now, and he advised Mr. Anchona to-night to employ some skilled New York detective, for he frankly confessed that he hadn't the least idea how to go to work to trace the girl in such a big city as New York."

"A sensible conclusion."

"So, by Straub's advice, Anchona to-morrow will put upon the track one of the best detectives in the country, and the lawyer says that if the girl is in the city the detective will surely find her."

"He must be a valuable man, this detective, for Straub is a cautious old coon, and is never very ready to recommend any one."

"The detective is called Carlton Brand."

"Brand?" and then Lee filled his glass nearly full of brandy and swallowed it at a gulp without winking.

"By Jove! you must be a deuce of a fellow to be able to put away the brandy in that style!" May observed, in evident admiration.

"Oh, that's nothing; I served my apprenticeship abroad, you know, where the natives disdain to water their liquor. So this detective — how do you call him?"

"Brand — Carlton Brand."

"An odd name, isn't it? And he is going to try his skill?"

"Yes; it is a very strange case. Anchona managed the matter so that neither his nor Straub's name should be known to the girl; therefore, when she arrived in New York, she could not hunt either one of them up, but as she knew she was to be met by some one, you would think she would go to the steamer office and inquire about the matter, particularly as she knew Mr. Blakely to be a warm friend — and he had assured her that if she needed any assistance, he would be glad to oblige her; at the steamer office, you know, she would be able to find out where he was."

"How do they know that the girl arrived in the city? Because she took the New York train is no proof that she continued in it until the city was reached."

"That idea occurred to Blakely, who seems to be a sensible, long headed fellow, and he followed the railroad clear from Branchport, where she took the train to New York, inquiring all along the line, but was not able to discover a clew to the girl — so it seems certain that she must have reached the city."

"The case excites my curiosity, although until the girl is found it does not matter to us. Her continued absence is our gain. By the way, about that will of Anchona's — is it signed yet?"

"It is."

"Suppose the girl is never found, to whom will the money go?"

"He will make a codicil, giving a share to different charities, and providing a little more liberally for Anita and myself."

"Let us hope the girl will not be found, then. You will be sure to keep me posted if anything new occurs?"

"Oh, yes."

Then the two indulged in a parting glass, and May withdrew, leaving Lee to brood over an idea that had entered his brain.

CHAPTER XVI.

THE chief of police sat in the office in a very unpleasant state of mind. Days had come and gone since Brand had set out to hunt down the mysterious assassin, and the only word that had been received from him was the request to send out a general alarm to arrest the woman known as Marita Madriea.

This had been promptly done; four-and-twenty hours had elapsed, but not the slightest clew had been gained in regard to the woman, neither had Brand been heard from.

As the superintendent meditated over the matter, inwardly heaping imprecations upon the head of the unknown villain, the mayor made his appearance.

"Anchona has been after me again," he explained. "He regards it as an outrage that the murderer of his brother has not been discovered, and really, superintendent, it seems strange to me that your men cannot get upon the track of the parties."

"Sit down," said the police official, placing a chair for his honor, "and just take a look at this; you will see that neither I nor my men have been idle."

And as he spoke he gave Brand's dispatch to the mayor.

"Aha! this looks like business!" his honor exclaimed, greatly gratified.

"Oh, yes; we're on the track now. It will take time, but in the long run I'll have the assassin."

"But this refers to a woman," the mayor remarked, after he had read the dispatch,

"Oh, yes."

"But you don't mean to say that the author or these mysterious murders is a woman?" exclaimed the amazed official. "It is not possible!"

"Oh, there's no doubt that the murderer is a man, but this party is evidently an accomplice. You know these rascals generally travel in gangs, and when one of the band is laid by the heels it usually results in the capture of the rest."

"Superintendent, you have really taken a load from any mind," the official exclaimed "I had begun to think that your new man would not make any more headway at the job than the poor fellow who was killed; and in fact, chief, so great a respect have I for the skill and cunning or this murderous assassin that I should have been far more willing to bet that he would ensnare the detective than that the detective would entrap him."

"It will take time, but we'll have him in the end," responded the superintendent in an oracular manner.

The mayor withdrew, perfectly satisfied with the assurance, and the chief smiled sarcastically as the door closed behind him.

"He thinks that the race is all over but the shouting," he muttered, "and I wish to Heaven it was, but it isn't. No news, they say, is good news, but I never found it so in police matters. Not hearing from Brand annoys me, I am afraid that he has come to a halt; the woman has succeeded in getting away, and that means that she must be smarter than lightning, or else Brand would have had her dead to rights long ago."

At this point his messenger came in with the intelligence that a gentleman desired to see him for a few minutes upon important business.

The chief gave orders to admit him, and soon a tall, distinguished-looking old gentleman made his appearance! He wore his iron-gray hair quite long, had very shaggy eyebrows that overhung the orbs beneath, and his gray beard swept low upon his breast.

He was attired in complete black, and jeweled rings of great value adorned his fingers. In brief, he was a fine specimen of the old-time gentleman, and the superintendent, who was a good judge of men, set him down for a foreigner.

"Have I the honah of addressing the chief of police, sah?" asked the gentleman, with courtly bow; and the instant he spoke, from the peculiar intonation, the superintendent guessed that he was a southerner.

"Yes, sir, I hold that office."

"I come to see you, sah, upon important business, but before I enter upon it, may I ask if our interview will be strictly private? Is there any danger of our conversation being overheard?"

"Not the slightest, sir; you can speak with perfect freedom."

The stranger was evidently an oddity, and the idea flashed into the superintendent's head that he might be a crank, but the chief was a wary bird and always prepared for unpleasant visitors who might become dangerous. He was seated at his desk, facing the stranger, and in a pigeon-hole under the top of the desk, convenient to his hand, was a cocked and loaded revolver.

"I am glad, sah, that such is the case, for what I have to say must not be heard by any ears but our own. I am from Terrebonne, Louisiana."

The superintendent bowed. The peculiarity of the man's speech was now explained. He was a Creole, and spoke with the old accent common to the southern of the extreme south.

"See, sah; what do you make of this?" continued the stranger, and he took from his pocket a bit of polished steel and laid it upon the desk.

At the first glance the superintendent thought it was a piece of a broken knitting-needle, but when he took it up, and the light of the gas played upon its polished surface, he saw that it was larger in diameter and of far superior quality of steel to that used for-knitting-needles. Then, too, it was blunt at one end, with signs of a fracture, showing that it had been broken, and the other end was drawn to a point as keen as the edge of a razor.

And as the chief glanced, inquiringly, at the shining steel, turning it around in his fingers, an idea of what it was dashed suddenly into his mind.

It was the broken blade of a dagger, or, more correctly speaking, poniard, as the small, fancifully-shaped daggers used by the southern races of Europe are termed, and by the means of just such a weapon all the victims of the mysterious assassin had come to their death.

The superintendent drew a long breath and surveyed his visitor with a glance that betokened uncommon interest.

Was this the secret slayer come in person to beard him?

"Well, well, sah, what think you of that toy?" asked the man, apparently growing impatient at the chief's silence.

"It is the broken blade of a dagger, I presume?"

"Right; a pretty little instrument, a fragile thing, and yet in the bands of a master, who knows where to strike, it will find and sap the life as surely as the largest blade that armorer ever forged."

"What is the idea of showing me this broken blade?"

"Can you not guess?" asked the other, in a theatrical elfort of way.

"I'm not good at conundrums."

"It is the weapon of the slayer who always strikes to kill," the southerner declared, becoming still more dramatic and mysterious in his manner.

"Is that so? I don't exactly understand; explain yourself!"

"Now you begin to talk business; how much is it worth?"

"That depends entirely upon the information you are able to give."

"This blade, tiny as it is, took the life of your best man."

"Brace?"

The southerner nodded.

"Now, my friend, since you know something about this matter, let me say to you that it is not a question of how much you can get for what information you may possess. You cannot drive a bargain with me after showing your hand in this manner. The possession of this bit of steel proves that you have a guilty knowledge of these outrageous crimes, and if you are not the principal you certainly must be an accomplice, and unless you make a clean breast of it, right away, I shall be under the disagreeable necessity of at once locking you up."

"Then Brand will be in danger," rejoined the man.

The chief started. Was it possible that the great detective had fallen into a snare?

"What's that you say?" he cried.

"I say if you lock me up a man about the size of Carlton Brand will be seriously incommoded," responded the other, in an entirely different voice, and then he laughed.

The superintendent stared in surprise. Even his keen eyes and shrewd wits had been at fault.

Brand himself stood before him.

"I wanted to try the effect of my get-up, chief," he explained; "and since it deceived you, I reckon that it will pass muster anywhere."

Then the detective sat down and related to the police official all that had occurred, and his plans for the future.

The consultation lasted until after twelve: the two left head-quarters together, and as they came out into the silent street they noticed a policeman, in full uniform, lying in the gutter in front of the building.

They hastened to him.

The man was stone dead.

Actuated by a sudden thought, Brand tore open his coat, vest, and shirt, and there, on his breast, right over the heart, was the tiny wound which had stolen his life away.

Again the secret assassin had stricken a deadly blow, and, in bold defiance, selected one of the best captains in the force, and then left the body in front of the police head-quarters.

It was a horrible mystery.

CHAPTER XXVII.

BLAKELY had been the sleuth-hound who had followed on
the track of the girl until he obtained a clew to the way
she had gone. But as we have seen, this clew could not be
followed to any decided results.

The girl was traced to the train; she boarded it, bound for
New York, and then disappeared as completely as though
she had vanished into thin air.

Blakely had hunted up the conductor who had charge of
the train that morning, but that official could not remember
anything about any such passenger as Miss Porras, although
as he frankly owned, unless there was something unusual
and striking about the lady's appearance, the chances were

that he would not have noticed her enough to recall the fact that she was on the train, particularly after a lapse of time.

Diligent inquiry among the railway officials in Jersey City produced no results, and at last Blakely was forces to seek Mr. Anchona and tell him that, as far as he was concerned, he could do no more, and then it was that the old lawyer advised the securing of the service of the experienced detective, Carlton Brand; but it took time to see Brand, for he was busy upon another case, as the reader is aware, and it was not until almost two weeks after the disappearance of the girl that any arrangement was made with him.

And now we will trace the girl's footsteps after she escaped from the fisherman's house.

She had determined to try to get out as soon as possible, and after the old woman retired with the dishes in which the simple meal was served, she set to work.

She discovered where the water had found its way into the cellar, a broken barrel-stave, fortunately at hand, served as a tool, and it was not a hard matter to dig a hole under the edge of the house, through which she crawled to the open air.

Then she fled as rapidly as possible, and, luckily, without attracting observation.

She walked straight on; in time, came to a railroad track, and followed it until she arrived at the depot, where she purchased a ticket for New York, exactly as the depot-master had described.

But in his statement to Blakely, the station-agent had made a slight mistake, but a mistake which threw the searcher off the track.

It was in regard to the day and train that the girl had taken.

She had gone on an afternoon train on Tuesday, and the man believed she had taken the first train on Wednesday.

Only a slight matter, apparently, and under ordinary circumstances it would not have made any difference, but this time it did.

The afternoon train ran off the track in crossing one of the numerous bridges that abound on the Long Branch railway, and the train crashed through the frail trestle work into the muddy stream below.

It was a fearful disaster. Happily for the passengers the water was not deep; if it had been, few of the three hundred odd travelers would have escaped to tell the tale.

But as it was, although assistance was near at hand, the people of the surrounding country flocking immediately to the aid of the sufferers, ten of the passengers were killed outright, while twenty were seriously injured, and among these unfortunate souls was our heroine.

She had been stunned by the shock, and when in a senseless condition taken out of the car, it was at first believed she was dead.

A careful examination disclosed the fact that life still remained, and although no wound appeared upon her delicate person; the doctors inclined to the belief that she had received serious internal injuries, and that her death was only a question of time.

Among the people who had hurried to the scene of the disaster, eager to be of assistance, was a middle-aged lady, who had been riding in a handsome barouche across the road-bridge over the stream, which was only a few hundred yards from the railway trestle, and had witnessed the train break through the structure. She was deeply interested in the beautiful girl, and listened for the doctor's opinion.

"She is pretty badly hurt, I'm afraid; yet still there may be a chance for her to recover, if she has immediate attention and careful nursing," was his statement.

"I'll take care of her, and see that she does not want for anything," the lady exclaimed. "My carriage is yonder, and if you will have her conveyed to it, I will take her home immediately, and send for my own family doctor."

The physician and the lady were well acquainted; and this offer took the doctor by surprise, for the lady was not apt to be liberal in her ideas.

Really glad, however, that a "change of heart" had taken place, the doctor caused the senseless girl to be conveyed to the carriage, and the lady drove off.

Her house was only a few miles away, being situated in the Little Silver Region, so-called from the small stream, the Little Silver River, which flows into the Shrewsbury. The lady was an odd character, one of the celebrities of the neighborhood, and deserves particular mention.

She belonged to the class popularly termed old maids, although in appearance she was far removed from the typical spinster, being tall and portly in person, with a really noble looking face, although it was marred by a stern and haughty expression.

Miss Edna Somerton she was called, and she had resided in the neighborhood for nearly twenty years, being one of the first of the city people to improve the neighborhood by building a magnificent house. She was wealthy, kept up a splendid establishment, and altogether was a person of great consequence in the vicinity.

She was respected and envied, but neither admired nor loved, for she did not court friendship of her neighbors, but was distant and haughty in the highest degree; inclined to misanthropy, too, and always bitter and sarcastic in her comments upon the world.

With a rod of iron she ruled her household, and, as a consequence, better-trained servants were seldom seen. The madam, as she was usually termed, was despotic; and while she was careful to deal justly with all with whom she came in contact, woe betide the man or woman who attempted to get the better of her in any way. To avenge an affront of this kind she would pour out her money like water; and her neighbors, who, like many of the cunning and grasping country folks, thought the city lady to be fair game, soon found to their sorrow that Miss Somerton was no one's fool, but, with her long purse and vindictive temper, was a most terrible person to affront.

That such a woman should, of her own accord, offer to take into her palatial mansion the injured girl — a perfect stranger, and one who seemed likely to die upon her hands, was an event that astonished everybody in the neighborhood.

Helena had suffered severely, but her injuries were far from being fatal, although for a week she lay in a critical state, being strictly forbidden by the doctor to speak or exert herself in any way, and thus it was that the ubiquitous reporters, who flocked to the scene of the accident like vultures to the banquet of blood, did not get her name and publish it in the list printed in all the daily journals of the sufferers by the calamity.

The madam watched over the girl with as much care as the most loving mother could give to an only daughter, and when at last the physician declared the critical moment had passed, and that there was no doubt of the girl's complete recovery, the joy that the mistress of the house felt could easily be seen.

The stern lines of her haughty face softened, and a softer light shone in her brilliant dark eyes.

The doctor, who had been Miss Somerton's family physician for years, was amazed at the interest she took in the girl, for he felt sure that she was a total stranger, although the madam had never said a word about the matter in any way.

After completing his examination, as he rose to depart, be remarked to Helena:

"We will soon have you up; you have improved wonderfully in four-and-twenty hours. All that is needed now is time and careful nursing, and you need not be afraid to talk a little. Not too much, you know, not enough to excite yourself, and the moment you feel you are becoming tired you must stop immediately."

"I will be careful, sir," the girl replied, in her low, flute-like voice.

"Oh yes, no doubt about that," Miss Somerton remarked, her imperious tones softening as she looked upon the helpless girl, "for a more obedient child than this poor girl was never seen."

Helena smiled gratefully, and the doctor could not refrain from a wondering look, for since he had been acquainted with the madam he had never known her to be so gracious.

Miss Somerton followed the doctor into the hall.

"She can converse now without any danger of it doing her an injury?"

"Yes, if she is careful not to overtax her strength."

"I'm glad of it, for I shall be able to find out something about her."

"She is a stranger, to you then, as I suspected?"

"Yes, a perfect stranger, and yet she seems as near and dear to me as if she was my own child. It's strange, isn't it? But then, you know, I'm an odd fish."

The doctor laughed and departed.

CHAPTER XXVIII.

AFTER the doctor's departure Miss Somerton returned to the invalid's apartment.

"Now, my dear, thank goodness you will be able to say something besides yes and no!" she exclaimed, as she drew an easy-chair up to the bedside and seated herself in it.

"It will be much more pleasant."

"And you have been very good, too; you have been perfectly resigned to hold your tongue for nearly two weeks, and yet the stupid men idiots are always protesting that it is an utter impossibility for a woman to refrain from talking," exclaimed the madam, with a sniff of contempt.

The invalid smiled at the earnestness of her hostess.

"And now that you are allowed to converse, you must satisfy my curiosity. I am a rather odd woman, I presume; everybody says that I am, and what everybody says must be true. I was riding over the road bridge when the railway accident occurred, and I reached the scene just in time to see you brought from the shattered car, more dead than alive. I don't know why it was, dear; I can't explain, even to myself, but something whispered to me that it was my duty to look after you, and as I am impulsive — too much so sometimes for my good — I yielded to the suggestion, and had you brought here. It was three days before you recovered use of your senses, and when the reporters called to get your name for publication I was unable to give them any satisfaction, and so in the report of the slaughter you were chronicled as an unknown. Doubtless your friends are puzzled to account for your absence."

"It is as I told you, madam, when you kindly offered to send to my friends that I was safe."

"I remember you said there wasn't any need of it — that there wasn't any one who would trouble themselves about your fate."

"It is the truth, madam; I could not explain more fully then, for the doctor positively prohibited me from saying a word more than was absolutely necessary."

"Very true."

"But now I can explain."

"Perhaps the explanation may not be a pleasant task," observed Miss Somerton, a sudden idea coming to her "You must not think, child, I am anxious to pry into your secrets. By some odd caprice I took a great interest in you as soon as I saw your face, and on the spur of the moment I determined that you should be well cared for, and if money could save your life, it should be saved. As to who and what you were, I never gave the matter a thought."

"I haven't anything to conceal, and, really, very little to relate; the story of my life is plain and uneventful; although there is something of a mystery connected with it," the girl replied , "My name is Helena Porras, and I was brought up in England, but I have an idea, from some careless, unguarded expressions, that at various times the lady who had charge of me let fall, that I am an American by birth. My mother I never knew, and I was told she died when I was only two years old. I was brought up in a little country village, about fifty miles from London. My father, who was a strange, silent man, always seeming oppressed by weighty cares, only came to see me at rare intervals. He was engaged in foreign commerce, I was told, and so was obliged to be abroad the greater part of the time. He was always kind, and seemed to greatly enjoy his visits to me.

"There was some mystery about him, for the lady, who was a childless widow, and who had taken care of me ever since I was an infant, knew no more about him than I did, and after each visit that my father made she would question me in regard to him, saying how strange it was that he did not seem to have any relatives or friends, and when he went away never left any address by means of which a communication could reach him.

"The bills were always settled promptly, and I provided with everything such as befitted the daughter of a gentleman of fortune — my education, in particular, being most carefully looked after.

"Just two months ago my father came to pay his usual visit, and I noticed that a great change had taken place; he was but the shadow of his former self, and when in my girlish anxiety I questioned him, he said he had been ill for quite a time, so much so that he had been obliged to give up his business, and the doctors said unless he relinquished all care the worst might be expected. Within a week he was prostrate on a sick bed, and soon the physicians announced that his case was hopeless, and warned him to prepare for death at any moment. Then, realizing that his end was near, he told me he had written to friends in America who would provide for me when he was taken away, which event soon took place. Ah, madam, it was a terrible affliction, for I had learned to love my father, and the blow fell upon me with horrible force."

Helena paused, emotion choking her utterance.

"Ah, yes; I can understand exactly how you felt, for I, too, have known what it is to have those near and dear to me torn away by the unrelenting hand of cruel fate."

And bending over the invalid, Miss Somerton pressed a soft kiss upon her forehead.

Thus encouraged, Helena conquered her emotion and proceeded with her story.

"A short time after my father's death, a letter arrived from New York, directed to me, and signed by a Mr. Fred Morecroft, attorney-at-law. It contained an order for a ticket to America, and directed me how to proceed. It stated that I would be met by a gentleman when the steamer landed;

who would look out for me until I could get something to do, as in the future I would have to depend upon my own exertions, as the person whom the writer represented — and who was evidently the one of whom my father spoke was not so situated as to be able to be of much assistance to me at present. It was a cold business letter, and it fairly chilled me when I read it. The lady, who had been as a second mother to me, was indignant at its tone, and advised me not to go, but, since I was dependent on myself for my support, to remain in England with her, as she felt sure I would get along better than by going abroad among strangers."

"You thought that you were in duty bound to obey your father's wish, though, and so you came."

"Yes, madam," and then Helena detailed the series of strange adventures which had befallen her since she arrived in New York bay, and with which the reader is already familiar.

Miss Somerton was amazed.

"Well, upon my word! I never heard of anything more astonishing in all my life!" she exclaimed. "Why, it is perfectly outrageous, and to think, you poor girl, that it was your fate to encounter such perils. It really seems as if fortune had a spite against you."

"And yet, madam, I have never done anything in all my life to deserve it."

"No doubt about that." the other exclaimed, "I flatter myself that I am an excellent judge of human nature, and if you haven't a good and innocent face, then I never saw one. But now, my dear — if you will excuse the question, considering the interest that I take in you — when you get well what do you propose to do? Will you go to the office of the steamship company and endeavor to find out the whereabouts of this gentleman — this Mr. Morecroft?"

"I suppose so, madam — I suppose this is the only course open to me."

"Oh, no, you are wrong there; if you do not choose you need not trouble the gentleman at all; you do not need any assistance from him. It is a very strange affair, and I must say there is something about it that I do not like. Why does the real party keep himself so carefully concealed? It looks to me as if your father labored under a misapprehension, when he intrusted you to the care of this person. He evidently thought that more would be done for you than simply paying your passage, and then leaving you to look out for yourself! Helena, my dear, I am a very plain-spoken woman; early in life I met with a great disappointment and it soured my temper — it made me hate all mankind. You are the first person to whom for thirty years my heart has at all warmed. I did not believe it possible that there was a creature in the world for whom I would ever care two straws, but, somehow, your face has softened my stubborn heart. I liked you at first, and now since you have been here, that liking has grown into love. If Heaven had been kind to me, and man true, it is possible that I would now have had a daughter like you to cheer me in the old age which is gradually creeping upon me. Helena, my darling, will you not stay here and be like a daughter to me? I am a rich woman, amply able to take care of you, amply able to give you the luxuries which such a girl as you are ought to have — your due by birth, I am sure.

"There is a vacant place in my heart — it had been there for many a long year, and I never dreamed that there was any one in this world could fill it — but now that the sunshine of your presence falls across my life, the void has disappeared, and I feel as I have not felt for years."

There were tears in the eyes of both of them at this point, for Helena, too, had been strangely attracted toward her hostess.

"I will send a trusty messenger to find out all about this Mr. Morecroft, and when it is done it will be an easy matter to ascertain who it is that is so anxious to conceal his identity. Then, child, if they can put forward a better claim to your love than I, you shall be free to go."

Helena's heart was so full that it was a difficult matter for her to express her thanks, and Miss Somerton quickly checked her when she made the attempt.

It was an odd occurrence, and, as the hostess said, the hand of Heaven seemed to be in it.

CHAPTER XXIX.

THE last daring crime on the part of the secret assassin filled the heart of the superintendent with unbounded rage.

"The infernal scoundrel!" he cried. "He dares to defy our power. Brand, this villain must be taken, no matter how much it costs or how great the toil; for if I can't capture him, the quicker I resign my office the better it will be for the city."

Brand agreed with the chief that at all hazards the assassin must be hunted down.

Another point, too, the superintendent and the detective agreed upon, and that was the annals of crime recorded no bolder or more remarkable rascal.

His bravado was wonderful. Instead of disposing secretly of the bodies of his victims, as is the usual custom of all murderers, he seemed to take a fiendish delight in leaving them in the most public places that could be selected, and how such a thing could be done without discovery by the police was a circumstance that puzzled the old and experienced heads of our two worthies.

The bodies must be transported to the locality where they were found by means of some vehicle, but how they were removed from the carriage to the ground without exciting notice was a mystery.

Diligent inquiry revealed the fact that a close carriage of some description — the officer who had encountered it on the corner was not exactly sure of the class — had come through the street about ten minutes before the time that the two had discovered the body.

There wasn't anything remarkable about the vehicle — nothing to attract the attention of the policeman, and so he had not favored it with a second glance.

His impression was that the carriage was a common hack with dark horses, but he was careful to state he wasn't at all sure about this, and the carriage might have been a coupe, drawn by a single horse; of two things he felt positive, though, the carriage was a close one and the animal — or animals — that drew it were dark in color.

This was a clew, although a faint one, and the chief proceeded to follow it up vigorously. He dispatched his keenest men to examine all the hacks in the city, and, by judicious "pumping," ascertain if any of the drivers knew aught of a coach, which had passed through Mulberry Street on a certain night at a certain hour.

Meanwhile, Brand proceeded according to his own ideas, having arranged with the superintendent a mode of communication, so that each could reach the other at almost any time.

The detective was now satisfied that he had made a mistake in endeavoring to entrap the assassin in his own proper person, but since his present disguise had deceived such an old familiar acquaintance as the superintendent, he felt certain that no one else would be able to penetrate it.

His plan was a simple one; for the third time he was going to try the scheme which had already been twice successful.

Brace, in the disguise of a wealthy stranger, had attracted the attention of the assassin and had fallen by his hand. He, Brand, had also succeeded, although in his case the woman, whom he had supposed in the Brace matter to be only a decoy, had apparently become the principal. He had escaped Brace's fate by a lucky chance, and now, armed with the knowledge which he had so unexpectedly gained, if he could succeed in inducing the assassin to mark him out for a victim, he felt satisfied he could make a capture.

This time Brand did not select the Fifth Avenue Hotel as a head-quarters. After the narrow escape that the vampire-like slayer had had in connection with that hotel, he did not think it likely it would be as good ground for his operations as some other of the fashionable up-town hotels. So he resolved to favor the Brevoort House with his patronage.

A week went by; Brand spent his money freely, cutting quite a dash and supporting the character of a wealthy creole sugar-planter from Southwestern Louisiana to the life, but never a bite did he have.

He was in constant communication with the chief and so kept posted in regard to the search for the mysterious carriage.

The superintendent succeeded no better than the detective, and was obliged to come to the conclusion that the carriage was a private one; so, with all the force that be could muster, he was endeavoring to make as close an examination of the private carriages in the city as he had made of the public ones, a task not easily accomplished.

Brand, on his part, since he had failed to attract his prey in the places which he had frequented, commenced to widen the scene of his operations.

"Possibly I have not paid attention enough to the nether side of New York life," he mused. "A southern planter with plenty of money, visiting the city for the purpose of enjoying himself, would be certain to see all the sights, particularly the ones that are only to be found after dark. The secret slayer seeks men with money in their purses, ergo, I must take pains to let all the world know that I am rolling in wealth."

To those who dwell within the gates of Gotham, and are possessed of the necessary funds, it is not a difficult matter to find guides to the lairs wherein the "tiger" lurks, ready to prey upon all who are rash enough to dare his claws and teeth.

Brand easily procured admission to all the high-toned gaming establishments, and in order to keep up his assumed character, be played with the reckless air of a man to whom money was no object.

For a week he kept this up, being nightly to be found at some one of the gilded gaming hells of the metropolis, and rarely returned to his hotel until three or four o'clock in the morning.

Numerous attempts were made by the well-dressed sharks, ever on the watch in such cities as New York for unsophisticated strangers, to obtrude themselves on the wealthy creole, but Brand, with his wonderful knowledge of the night-birds of the city, quickly perceived that they were mere vulgar rascals, and not the big game he sought.

Brand being a man of ice, never allowed the excitement of play to influence him in the least, and, as is a general rule in this life, fortune smiled upon his game; the blind goddess being noted for favoring the indifferent souls who rather scorn than seek her smiles.

Luck favored him so much that the gaming-house keepers began to hate the very sight of his tall and handsome figure.

One particular night, the eighth one that Brand had devoted to this quest, an odd incident occurred.

The detective, about midnight, had strolled into what was properly called the "boss" gaming-house of the city, a palatial brown-stone mansion on Twenty-third Street, where the largest game in the metropolis was played, and which admitted within its walls only the high-toned sports of the city.

Representative men, bankers, lawyers, politicians, and the young bloods who possess more money than brains, lounged in the sumptuously-furnished parlors, discussing the topics of the day, or partook of the elaborate lunch which was served regularly at twelve o'clock, flanked with the finest wines and liquors, all free as air to the patrons of the house.

The Bon Ton Club the place was called, and those who were not in the secret supposed it to be a club-house pure and simple, while in reality it was nothing but a regular gaming-hell.

This night Brand was out of sorts. He began to feel annoyed that he had not succeeded in getting upon the trail of his prey, and the question arose in his mind if he had not better adopt some other plan than the one he was pursuing.

He was engaged in mentally debating this subject when he sat down to play, and so for some little time he made his bets hap-hazard, paying little attention as to how the game was going.

There was a slender, dark-faced young man on his right hand as he sat down, and Brand noticed that he looked like a foreigner and was evidently deeply interested in the game, betting heavily, and, as the detective perceived in a short time, with decidedly bad luck.

The cards ran out, the board was cleared of the chips; a fresh pack, after being duly shuffled, was placed in the dealing-box, and again the "Make your game, gentlemen," of the dealer was heard.

The dark young man put a hundred dollars' worth of chips on the king, and Brand, in the jargon of the gamblers, 'coppered' the king with fifty dollars' worth of chips to lose.

This action instantly excited the stranger. With flashing eyes and a voice hoarse with suppressed passion, yet modulating his tone so as not to excite the attention of any of the gamesters, he turned to Brand and said:

"What do you mean by that? Do you desire to cast a spell of ill-luck upon me? Do you 'copper' the card with fifty to lose just because I bet a hundred that it would win?"

"Your action sir, in betting upon the card had nothing in the world to do with mine. You think it will win — I think it will lose: that is all there is to it," Brand replied, calmly, thinking the young man had allowed the excitement of the moment to get the better of his judgment.

"I have not won a stake since you came to the table, and you have bet against me in the most persistent manner. If the king loses there will be trouble between us!" the other cried.

CHAPTER XXX.

THE superstition of gamblers is proverbial, and Brand would have been inclined to laugh at the incident, if the face and tone of the young stranger had not betrayed how deeply earnest he was about the matter.

The detective had been playing with so little interest that he had not been conscious of betting in direct opposition to his neighbor and nothing was further from his thoughts than the idea of so doing with any malicious purpose.

But now that his attention was aroused, he immediately discovered why the young man's anger had been excited.

His stack of chips was gone; the few ten-dollar checks which he had bet upon the king were all that he possessed, and Brand remembered now that when he had taken his seat at the table there was quite a pile of checks — five or six hundred dollars' worth at the least — in front of his neighbor.

Fortune had frowned upon him, and with the usual inconsistency of man he was disposed to attribute his ill-luck to Brand's presence.

With decided interest now the detective watched the game. He had got the idea into his head that the king would lose just because the young man appeared to be so anxious that it should win.

Brand was something of a fatalist, and he thought he had noticed that when a man gets into a streak of bad luck it generally lasts some time, and the more one struggles against it the worse it becomes.

This was the gambler's superstition over again.

"No use bucking against the game when luck runs dead opposite!"

The king came out — a losing card — and the young man's chips went to "join the majority" on the dealer's side.

A stifled curse came from the stranger, but with the exception of the strange glitter in his dark eyes and a curious way in which he compressed his lips, he betrayed no signs of the passion which was raging within his veins.

He touched Brand on the shoulder, and whispered in his ear:

"Will you have the kindness to come outside, so that I can have the pleasure of a few minutes' conversation with you?"

The man's tone was calm — polite even, and yet Brand detected that there was a tone of menace in it.

"Certainly." he replied, for the detective was not the man to back out of a game of this sort when it was forced upon him. "Just wait until I cash in these checks."

"I'm in no hurry, sir," and the man cast an envious glance at the pile of checks before the detective as he spoke.

Brand had commenced with twenty checks, worth five dollars apiece, and in the short time that he had been playing had won quite a little stack, so when he cashed them in, four hundred and eighty dollars were counted out to him in place of the one hundred he had originally invested.

"Quite a snug little sum for an hour's work," the detective murmured, as he stowed away the money in his pocket-book, "or an hour's amusement, rather." he added. "But if I had needed the money the odds are a thousand to one that I would not have been able to secure it, and that is the way the world goes."

While Brand had been attending to this business, the stranger had gone to the elaborate sideboard, where the liquors were displayed, and helped himself to a small tumbler of brandy, which he drank with as much ease as though it were only water.

Down the stairs the two went, the young man leading the way, through the carefully-guarded portals, for there were three vigilant guards to pass before admittance could be gained to the club-room, and then out into the street.

It was a bright moonlight night, and the street, thanks to the moon and the gas, was almost as light as day.

When the pair gained the pavement the stranger turned and faced Brand, anger appearing in every feature.

"I suppose you are aware, sir, that your cursed interference in my affairs has cost me a pretty penny to-night?" he cried.

"No, I am not aware of it," the detective replied, regarding the stranger curiously, for such men were a study to this human bloodhound, and then, too, now that he was taking the trouble to examine the features of the other closely, the idea came to him that he had seen just such a face before; but, for the life of him, he could not tell where, and this puzzled Brand, for he prided himself, and with good reason, upon his excellent memory. It was seldom that a face once seen by him was ever forgotten, or the circumstances under which it was brought to his notice.

"Do you know what I have lost to-night in that infernal den?" and the speaker shook his clinched fist fiercely at the palatial mansion, that looked far more like the abode of a merchant prince than a gambling hell, within whose devouring maw hundreds of victims were sacrificed weekly.

"My dear sir, I do not take the slightest interest in the recital of your losses, so I trust you will have the kindness to refrain from inflicting the tale upon me," Brand remarked, with cold indifference. "Only I will observe that a man who goes into a tiger's den of his own free will, with the idea of securing the teeth and claws of the animal that he may carry them away and exhibit them as trophies, has no right to grumble if the beast proves the victor in the struggle, and all he has to show for his pains are some ugly scratches. If you can't afford to lose you had no business to play, and if I was in the preaching line of business, I should remark that it is a great moral lesson for you, young man; go! and sin no more!"

"You infernal scoundrel!" hissed the other between his firm-set teeth, "It is all your fault."

"You are crazy, young man, and so I refrain from becoming angry at your abusive expressions, but I warn you that my patience has its limits, and if you do not keep a watch over that unruly tongue, I may be forced to give you a lesson in manners."

"You give me a lesson?"

"Yes, my friend — teach you how to behave yourself."

"You are relying upon your superior physical gifts, or else you would not dare to threaten me."

"And you are relying upon the fact that your size protects you, or else you would never have dared to let your tongue wag as freely as it has," Brand retorted. "If you were a man of my own weight and inches I would have pulled your nose the moment you dared to apply an abusive name to me."

"You would have pulled my nose!" cried the other, his face distorted with passion, and his hands clinched in a manner strongly indicative of war.

"Yes, sah, in two wags of a goat's tail, and I give you fair warning that if you should again forget yourself and affront me in that ungentlemanly way, despite my age, and the dignity which should attach to it, I shall immediately proceed to take some measures which may be decidedly unpleasant to you. Although I have the advantage of superior size and weight, yet you have youth as a counterbalance, but for all that I will try a dog-fall with you if you willfully provoke me to the encounter."

Brand was a marvelous actor, and this assumption of the manner of a dignified yet irate southerner was perfection.

The young man drew himself up proudly.

"I am a gentleman, sir, and I presume that you are also one."

"The man who doubts the truth of that statement, as far as I am concerned, sah, will get himself into trouble."

"As we are both gentlemen, we must not descend to fisticuffs, as if we were only a pair of coal-heavers."

"Correct, sah; but when a man provokes me into a quarrel I am ready to meet him with any kind of weapons, from ten-pound rifle-cannons down to pop-guns!"

"Stay a moment!" the young man exclaimed, haughtily. "It is not I who have provoked this quarrel, but you."

"Sah, you are entirely mistaken; I don't know anything about you, and have not the slightest desire to make your acquaintance. If you had got up from the table and gone away without saying anything to me I never would have known that you existed at all. But you are a donkey, sah; you have lost your money, and you wish to throw the blame upon some one else."

"Enough of this!" cried the young man, fierce in passion. "Are you man enough to make your words good — do you dare to meet me with suitable weapons?"

"Anything you like, my deah boy! Although I am not as young as I might be, yet I flatter myself you will find me game to the backbone."

"Can you handle a sword?"

"Try me, and find out!" For mere sport Brand was going to see the matter through.

"I give you fair warning that I am an expert swordsman. I was the best man of my class at Heidelberg, in Germany, when I was at college, and I have a pair of rapiers that I brought home with me when I returned: they are at your service."

"And I give you fair warning that I had as lief spit you on a German rapier as on any other weapon in the known world!" Brand blustered.

"Come, then! I know where I can get a boat, and under the Weehawken cliffs we will not be disturbed!"

"Go ahead, sah!" the disguised detective responded.

CHAPTER XXXI.

STRAIGHT toward the river they went, stopping only once on the way to enable the young man to enter a small, old-fashioned brick house, where he said he lodged, and from which he speedily reappeared, bearing under his arm a pair of swords carefully wrapped in flannel cases, so that any one not posted in regard to them would never have been apt to suspect what they were.

No further words were exchanged between them until they reached the street which ran parallel with the water.

Turning to the north, they went on for about a dozen blocks, then halted at a small "all-night" restaurant, whose sign declared "we never close."

"The man who runs this place keeps the boats also," the young man remarked. "He will not think it strange that I come at such a time as this for a craft, for often in the small hours of the night, when my brain burns with study, I take a pull on the river, and so keep myself from going mad."

Brand took a good glance at the speaker, and the reflection came to his mind that if he was not a trifle crazy now, he could not boast of any more sense than the law allows.

"It will only take a moment to get the oars and key to unlock the padlock which fastens the boat." the young man continued, halting with his hand on the latch of the door.

"All right, sah, I will wait for you," the detective replied, still keeping up his assumed character. But when the door of the saloon closed behind the other Brand began to seriously reflect upon the situation.

"This fellow is a little cracked in the upper story, and I begin to believe that I have made a donkey of myself by being drawn into this quarrel," he murmured. "I thought the fellow was an impudent and arrogant puppy, and was just in the right state of mind to vent my spleen upon him. I have had such deuced ill-luck in this case that my temper has really become soured, and I thought I might work off a little of my ill-humor on him, but the affair is getting serious. The fellow may be a better swordsman than I am, although I doubt it, and it would be the toughest kind of a joke if he should succeed in spitting me.

"And I don't want to kill the lunatic, either, for by so doing I would get myself in a regular hole, but, hang me, if I don't see the affair through now that I have become mixed up in it."

The return of the dark-browed stranger with a pair of oars on his shoulder and a padlock key in his hand put a stop to Brand's cogitations.

Without a word he led the way across the street to the dock.

The moon afforded ample light.

By the side of the pier, which extended into the river, a flight of rude steps led to a landing raft to which a half dozen boats were fastened.

The stranger unlocked one and placing oars in its motioned Brand to embark.

"The tide is coming in, with a strong flood, and it will be an easy task to reach our destination," he remarked. "I will take the oars, if you haven't any objection, for I presume I am better acquainted with the spot to which we are going than you."

"Oh, yes, no doubt about that, sah, for I don't know anything about it at all, but still it seems to me that it is hardly fair to allow you to exhaust yourself by rowing, while I remain perfectly fresh for the encounter."

"Do not trouble yourself in regard to that; my muscles are like iron and my sinews strong as steel; besides, if I did not tame the fire that burns within my veins by this slight exercise, I would be apt to kill you so quickly that there would not be any pleasure in the encounter."

And this opinion was delivered in such a matter-of-fact way that it caused even the old and experienced detective to draw a long breath, indicative of great amazement.

By this time the two were in the boat; the young man applied himself to the oars and a few strokes carried them out clear of the pier to the bosom of the stream.

As the rower had said, the tide was making it strong, and as the stranger was evidently a practiced oarsman, rowing a long and powerful stroke with seeming ease, to reach the Weehawken shore was not a difficult task.

"Now we shall soon see, what we shall see," remarked the young man, sententiously. "But that reminds me: we have not yet made each other's acquaintance. Suppose we go through with the ceremony of an introduction? You have some worldly affairs, of course, to settle. All men have, particularly when they are of your age; your time on earth being limited, suppose you confide any important matters to me? I will faithfully attend to the trust when you are no more."

"Confound it, young man," the detective exclaimed, really nettled by the assurance of the other, yet careful not to betray himself by departing in a single iota from the character he had assumed. "You haven't got me dead and buried already, you know! Don't you think that you are rather previous in your remarks? You'll find out before we get through, I reckon, that you haven't got half so sure a thing as you think. And as for being any better acquainted than we are at present, I will tell you, frankly, that I don't care two cents who you are, and it isn't any of your business who I am, but don't fool yourself with the idea that my grave is ready, and all you have to do is to put me into it!"

"But it is ready; after I have slain you I shall cast your body into the river," the other replied, calmly. "This smooth tide, over whose glassy surface we are now gliding, will cover all traces, and when the waters in time give you up, you will go upon record as another stranger found dead, by hands and means unknown."

A glance of fire shot from Brand's eyes, and it was only by a strong effort that he retained his composure.

He suspected that the stranger was the mysterious assassin.

CHAPTER XXXII.

"HE has the eyes of a fiend," Brand murmured, communing with himself, as he narrowly watched the face of the oarsman. "But unless he is a far better swordsman than he is likely to turn out to be, I'll cook his goose for him."

Although it was years since Brand had handled the foils in the Turn Halle, be was not at all rusty, for as fencing had alway been a passion with him, during his trip to foreign land, he had engaged in friendly bouts with some of the best swordsmen of both Europe and Brazil, and so had at his fingers' ends the latest and most cunning tricks of the masters of "carte and tierce."

When they arrived within a couple of hundred yards of the Weehawken shore, the rower rested on his oars for a moment, and allowed the boat to drift along with the tide, while he cast a glance around,

"Aha!" he ejaculated, in a satisfied tone, "I thought I could hit the spot just suited for such an affair as the one in which we are engaged. We will settle our quarrel in the exact place where Alexander Hamilton fell by the hand of Aaron Burr."

And Brand, glancing at the shore, saw that his companion had conducted him to the locality where it was commonly believed the fatal duel between the rival statesmen had taken place.

"It doesn't make a picayune's difference to me, sah," the disguised detective replied. "I don't care a button who fought and fell; all I want is about six squar' feet of level ground, and if I don't give you a dose that will last one while, then you are welcome to take my head for a football."

"If you have prayers to say, speak them before we cross swords, for you will not have a chance afterward," the other rejoined.

Then, with a few oar-strokes, he drove the boat to the shore.

Leaping out, he drew the bow up on the little stretch of beach, tucked the swords under his arm, and, clambering over the rocks, proceeded to where a narrow shelf of level land jutted out from the steep side of the Palisades, as the rocky formation that frowns upon the western bank of the placid Hudson is called.

When the level space was reached the young man faced about, drew the swords from their covering, and in the ceremonious manner of the fencing-room, tendered them to Brand.

A single glance revealed to the experienced eyes of the detective that there wasn't the least difference between the two weapons; a better pair of "slogger" blades, as the cut and thrust, edge and point dueling tools of the German students are termed, Brand had never seen.

Selecting one, the detective stepped back a couple of paces, and whirled the keen blade through the air, cutting a figure eight with much ease as though it were but a toy.

His antagonist looked on with a scowl; being an expert swordsman himself he detected from the manner in which Brand handled the weapon that he had no mean antagonist to encounter.

"It was not a boast, then; you do know something of the weapon," he observed.

"Do you suppose I would have been fool enough to have allowed myself to be bullied into coming with you if I didn't?" the detective retorted.

"But I will kill you for all that!" the other cried, fiercely advancing as he spoke, and lunging straight at Brand's breast; but the detective was on his guard, for like a wary swordsman he had kept watch of his opponent's eyes, and from them received ample warning of the attack.

With the firmness of a rock Brand received the onset; there was a flash of steel in the air as he parried the thrust, and then, as the rashness of the attack had thrown his antagonist out of "distance," there was a quick straightening of the detective's supple arm, followed by a cry of rage from the stranger.

The point of the detective's blade had pierced his antagonist's shoulder.

"Not so very rusty, after all, you perceive, my friend," Brand remarked, as the other recoiled, gasping with rage. "Bah! you are nothing but a bungler — you uncovered yourself at the first thrust! I might just as easily have sent my blade through your lungs, and finished the affair at a single stroke, as to prick you in the shoulder. You know enough of the sword to understand that, I presume?"

"Well, why did you not do so?"

"Because I don't want to kill you; that isn't my game."

"No? What is it, then?"

"To make you a prisoner; carry you back to the city and introduce you to some gentlemen who are extremely anxious to make your acquaintance."

"Anxious to make my acquaintance! I am at a loss to comprehend your meaning."

"Why, it is as plain as the moon shining in the sky yonder. You laid a trap, and, as often happens in this uncertain life, were the first to get caught. It is the old story of the engineer hoist by his own petard."

Then, with a quick movement, Brand removed his wig and beard and stood revealed in his own proper person.

An expression of the most intense amazement appeared upon the face of the stranger. Dropping the point of his sword to the ground, he stared like one transfixed with wonder.

Brand was disappointed. This was not the expression that he had expected to produce.

"You are not an old man, then?" his antagonist remarked, wonderingly.

"Not much, and there is where your calculations were out of joint. You picked me up for a victim, but the supposed pigeon has turned into a hawk."

"I do not understand your meaning. Why should I select you for a victim — who are you and what is the meaning of this singular disguise?"

The detective took a good look at his questioner before he made reply, and the thought came to him that if the other was the man he took him to be, then most certainly he was a complete master of the art of dissimulation.

"My name is Brand — Carlton Brand, the detective."

"Ah, I can understand you being disguised, and I regret that I interfered with you; possibly I have disarranged your plans."

"Not at all; you are the man for whose express benefit I assumed the disguise."

"You are clearly laboring under some mistake," replied the other, incredulously.

"Oh, no, you are my mutton! so throw down your toasting-fork and I will snap the bracelets on you," and Brand drew from his pocket a pair of handcuffs which he dangled in the air.

"You are crazy? What charge do you bring against me?"

"Murder!" replied Brand, sternly.

CHAPTER XXXIII.

"Ha, ha, ha!" laughed the young man, and the rocks gave back the shrill and rather discordant sound.

"Murder! how absurd and how extremely like, this situation, to the climax of a soul-harrowing romance. I am the criminal hunted down and you the expert detective — the bloodhound who has shadowed me to my doom — ha, ha, ha!" and again he laughed.

Now Brand felt sure that he was in the right track, for his quick ears detected that there was something false and unnatural about the merriment of the other.

"And you are going to put those pretty little ornaments upon my wrist, eh?" the unknown continued, this time in a bantering tone; "going to carry me back to New York and exhibit me as a specimen of your skill in the detective line. But come, enough of this nonsense. Do you suppose that I will tamely submit to such an outrage?"

"You will be obliged to submit, for you can't help yourself," retorted the detective.

"Bah!" and with the utterance of the contemptuous exclamation he flung his sword straight at Brand's head, and then plucked from a secret pocket in the breast of his coat a revolver, evidently a self-cocker, for he discharged it immediately.

Crack, crack, crack, rung out the sharp reports on the still night air; three shots, fired point-blank at Brand's breast as fast as the cylinder could revolve.

The detective was in a measure taken by surprise; for although from the expression in the eyes of the other he had anticipated an attack, yet he had counted upon its being made with the sword, and the sudden production of the revolver was unexpected.

He was quick to follow the example of his antagonist, but before he could get his pistol out the bullets of his foe took effect.

Each one of the three shots struck him — he staggered back and then fell on his knees.

A yell of triumph came from the unknown. Taking deliberate aim at Brand's head he fired a fourth shot.

The detective fell over sideways.

Then satisfied that he had disabled his powerful antagonist, he approached with the idea of administering the final stroke.

But Brand half rose, evidently badly hurt and partially stunned, yet sensible of what was going on, leveled his revolver and fired.

A cry of rage came from the other as the bullet tore through his flesh, and he recoiled before his determined foe.

Brand staggered to his feet, the blood streaming from the wounds in his head, presenting a frightful sight.

"Dead or alive, I'll hold you," he gasped.

The young man answered with another shot, which cut a lock of hair from the detective's temple.

And then again the flash came from the revolver of the man-hunter, as he advanced with dogged resolution upon his prey.

Again the bullet had hit its mark.

The unknown had emptied his revolver, and so was weaponless.

With a yell of anger he threw the now useless weapon at the head of the detective.

The aim was good, and the missile tumbled Brand over upon his back.

The young man sprung forward to improve the advantage, but as he came up to Brand, the detective quickly raised his arm and sent another bullet into the person of his foe.

Again a yell of mingled rage, and then, apparently panic-stricken, the unknown turned and fled toward the boat.

He was bleeding from the wounds that he had received, but evidently not one of them was severe enough to disable him.

By the time he was half-way to the boat the detective had managed to regain his feet, and opened fire on the retreating man, but his wounds had rendered his aim uncertain, and although the bullets whistled closer to the person of the fugitive than was agreeable to that gentleman, yet he managed to get into the boat and push off into the stream.

Brand pursued him with grim determination.

One revolver being emptied of its charges, he drew another and kept up the fire, although growing so weak from his wounds that he could hardly stand.

The fugitive bent to his oars with all his strength.

"This man is a demon," he muttered between his firm-set teeth.

Shot after shot the desperate detective sent after the retreating boat. He had clambered to the top of a huge rock that jutted out into the water so as to secure a better aim, but venturing too far out slipped upon the slimy surface, lost his balance, and went headlong into the water.

The hunted man uttered a cry of joy upon perceiving this unexpected stroke of misfortune.

"Ah, you bloodthirsty sleuth-hound, that puts a stop to your target-practice for a time at least!"

He brought his boat around and rowed back to the point from whence he had started, by so doing of course bringing his back to the shore, but he was careful to glance over his shoulders every now and then for the purpose of noting if Brand had arisen from the water.

But he was not gratified by a sight of the man-hunter.

He brought his boat alongside the rock from which the detective had slipped into the water.

It was quite deep at that point, and the current was strong.

"He would have been swept up stream for some distance in such a strong flood tide as this," the searcher murmured. "I must look for him up the stream. By this time, unless he has received a mortal hurt, he must have risen to the surface, and if I do not succeed in finding him, then I ought to be easy in my mind about the matter, for it will be pretty conclusive evidence that he has found a grave in the restless waters."

Keeping the boat a short distance from the shore, he rowed slowly along up the river.

His quest was in vain; not a vestige of the detective could he discover.

Fully an hour he spent in the search, and then, satisfied that nothing could be gained by devoting more time to it he headed his boat across the river to the New York shore.

"Brand is dead, beyond a doubt," he mused. "But oh! what wouldn't I give if I could only be sure of it! One look at his lifeless body would be worth a fortune."

He feared the detective more than all the world beside.

CHAPTER XXXIV.

Miss Somerton was as good as her word in regard to the promises that she had made to the girl who had come under her roof in so strange a manner.

She carefully wrote down all the facts appertaining to the case, and then sent a message summoning a gentleman whose kind offices she desired to enlist in the matter.

This person was no other than Mr. Lee. Miss Somerton had made his acquaintance some two years before the time of which we write, and there wasn't any one in the world for whom she had a higher respect. In fact, the regard that the pair had for each other once excited considerable gossip in the circle in which they moved, and the rumor had been widely circulated that it would result in a match, despite the difference in their ages.

And gossip in this instance was not so far out of the way, for the gentleman had been most decidedly attracted by the lady, and if it had depended upon him, no doubt he would have become her lord and master.

But Miss Somerton, while frankly admitting that if she was twenty years younger her answer might be different, resolutely declined.

"No, no," she said; "I am in the sere and yellow leaf, while you are merely on the threshold of manhood. Possibly the great difference in our ages may not be so apparent now, but just wait until twenty years have gone by; then I shall be a decrepit old woman, tottering on the verge of the grave, while you will be in the very prime of life. Besides, there has been one love in my life, and the remembrance of the anguish that it caused me is still fresh in my memory. Remain my constant, faithful friend, and do not dream of ever being aught else."

And this was the only relationship that existed between the two, all gossip to the contrary being utterly unfounded.

So when he was summoned the young man came at once.

When the situation was explained to him, he accepted the commission.

"Certainly," he said; "I will give the matter instant attention."

Miss Somerton had merely said that there was a young lady under her care about whose friends seemed to be some mystery, and she wished to have the matter investigated.

And now that the gentleman had accepted the commission, she produced the memoranda she had made.

He opened the paper and perused it carefully, and the surprise he experienced was so great that it was with much difficulty — despite the great command he had over himself — that he refrained from betraying it.

Miss Somerton's *protegee* was the girl who had so mysteriously disappeared, and she had succeeded in avoiding all search, although the banker paid out money as freely as so much water in the endeavor to discover her hiding-place.

"It's a strange affair," observed the lady, misunderstanding the expression upon the face of her guest.

"Yes, very strange; but I think I can easily ascertain all about the matter. It ought not to be difficult."

And then as he spoke, to his mind came a strange suspicion. Might it not be possible that in some way, his connection with the affair had been discovered? Was not this task which Miss Somerton had confided to him a shrewd device to ascertain exactly how he stood? It was improbable and yet not impossible. May had betrayed the banker to him; why might not the informer play the traitor again and betray him to the banker?

It was a wild idea, and yet so strangely was the wily schemer constituted, that he allowed himself to give serious heed to it.

He did not believe that Miss Somerton was a party to any attempt to lead him into a trap, but thought she might be duped into playing the part of a tool.

His first idea was to ascertain if there had been any communication between the lady and the banker. They were not acquainted, as far as he knew.

"By the way, Miss Somerton," he remarked, after a moment's pause, during which he had been revolving these ideas in his head, "have you heard the latest gossip?"

"No; I have almost retired from society, and so I hear very little."

"Ah! then I suppose I must make a confession, but I thought you had heard something of it. Rumor declares that before long my bachelor days will be over."

"Allow me to congratulate you, then, if the report is correct," she said, in the kindest manner.

"I fear I must plead guilty to the soft impeachment."

"Who is the lady? Do I know her?"

"I am not certain as to that, although I think it is probable. She is the daughter of the banker, Juan Anchona."

A quick, convulsive breath came from the white lips of the lady; her face grew pallid and for a moment it seemed as if she was about to faint.

The gentleman sprung from his seat in alarm, but she waved him back.

"It is nothing — a sudden faintness, that is all," she murmured, speaking with great difficulty.

"Shall I not ring for your maid?" he inquired, perceiving that he had unwittingly caused the lady mental pain.

"No, no, it is over now, but the shock was so sudden, so entirely unexpected, that for the moment all the painful past was recalled to me and the old wound reopened. I have not heard that name for years."

"You are acquainted with the banker, then?" Lee asked, perceiving that in endeavoring to clear up one mystery he had stumbled upon another.

"Yes, I was acquainted with him once, twenty years ago, and at his hands I suffered an injury from which I shall never recover while life remains."

The tone in which she spoke was full of bitterness, and it was plain that although years had elapsed the remembrance of her wrong was still fresh in her recollection.

"You really astound me, Miss Somerton!"

"No doubt, for I have always been as dumb as a marble woman as far as my wrongs were concerned, but now since I have betrayed myself and excited your curiosity, it is only right that I should gratify it. It is a brief and broken tale, with a mystery that even I have never been able to solve.

"Are you aware that Mr. Juan Anchona had a brother William Anchona?"

"No," answered the gentleman. "The only brother of whom I have any knowledge was called Jose and resided in Texas."

"Yes; I knew that there was a Jose Anchona, and that he went south in quest of fortune, when quite a boy; he was the second brother. Juan was the eldest and William the youngest. Juan and William were in business together twenty years ago and both of them suitors for my hand.

"I preferred the youngest, and I believed I loved him as sincerely as ever a man was loved. Although the brothers were rivals it did not seem to breed strife between them.

"Juan took his brother's success in a good-natured way, wished him all possible happiness and congratulated me on my choice.

"I, believing him to be in earnest in what he said, looked upon him as a noble-hearted brother. Little did I dream then that he was but a snake in the grass, and that all the time he was wishing me happiness he was secretly plotting to render me forever wretched.

"My wedding-day was fixed, and on the very night before it William Anchona disappeared as utterly as though the grave opened and swallowed him.

"I was nearly crazy; Juan Anchona pretended to be equally alarmed, but he did not deceive me, for even in my excited state I was acute enough to perceive that his alarm was not genuine.

"The most vigorous search was absolutely fruitless; not a single trace of William Anchona, either alive or dead, could be discovered.

"Time passed on, and thinking that I had forgotten the vows I had sworn, Juan Anchona renewed his suit, only to be driven from my presence in anger, for I plainly told him that I suspected he had a hand in his brother's disappearance.

"All the defense he made was that William was unworthy my love, and it was a fortunate thing for me that the union had not taken place.

"Since that time I have never set eyes upon any of the Anchona family. I have heard that Juan has prospered and become a wealthy man: but mark my words, Mr. Lee, if he is guilty of injuring his brother the truth will come out some day."

"I am glad that you confided in me, for in my new relation to Mr. Anchona I may be able to ascertain the truth: but I cannot believe that you are right in your surmise that he injured his brother in any way, although there is evidently a dark mystery connected with the affair. And I will not rest until I have solved it."

CHAPTER XXXV.

AFTER a few more words of unimportant conversation, Helena was summoned and introduced to Mr. Lee, and Miss Somerton, who watched to see what impression her *protegee* would produce upon the gentleman, perceived that it was decidedly favorable, but she was puzzled by the girl's behavior, for never before had she seen Helena act so strangely, and she took occasion when they retired to robe for dinner to question her.

"Indeed, I cannot understand why it is that this gentleman's presence affects me so strangely," Helena replied. "He is a stranger to me; I have never met him before to my knowledge, and yet his face seems familiar and a feeling of alarm fills my breast all the time that I am in his presence."

"But why should you feel alarmed?" demanded Miss Somerton, amazed at this disclosure.

"I cannot explain that — there isn't the least reason why I should feel so, for he seems to be an agreeable, pleasant gentleman. The sentiment is one of those inexplicable things which cannot be explained. If I was inclined to be superstitious, I should believe that in the future Mr. Lee will prove to be my enemy and strive to work me harm, and that the fear with which he now inspires me is the warning of a subtle instinct latent in my nature."

Miss Somerton shook her head; she was completely puzzled. For Mr. Lee she had the highest respect and she could not bring herself to believe that there was any foundation for the girl's suspicion, and this much she said to Helena.

"Oh, Miss Somerton!" the girl exclaimed, "do not think for an instant that I attach any importance to my foolish and baseless imaginings. I was only trying to account for them, that was all; but I was silly to speculate upon the matter; why, one might as well try to soberly analyze a dream."

The hostess nodded her head as much as to say that this was her opinion also, but in reality she was much more troubled about the matter than she was willing to confess, for she was rather inclined to be superstitious, being quite apt to allow her instinct to sway her judgment, particularly in regard to new acquaintances.

Nothing more was said upon the subject, but when they met the gentleman at dinner, Miss Somerton was particular to notice all that passed.

Helena tried her utmost to appear pleasant and unconcerned, but, in spite of her endeavors, the hostess could perceive a weight of apprehension sat heavily upon her soul.

And once or twice, Miss Somerton fancied she detected that Lee was also keeping a covert watch upon the girl, and this excited her suspicions.

"Can it be possible that these two are not strangers to each outer?'" she thought. "Can it be that they have met before and something unpleasant has passed between them?"

But the hostess was not willing to harbor this suspicion, for, so doing, it would imply that Helena had purposely deceived her, and so great was her trust in the girl that she would have been willing to stake her life upon her truthfulness.

"If they have met, the knowledge has passed from the girl's memory."

To this conclusion came the hostess by the time the repast was finished, and they adjourned to the veranda to enjoy the balmy breeze blowing from the ocean.

Hardly were they comfortably seated, when, through the gathering gloom of the dusky evening, an odd, strange figure came shambling up the walk from the front gate.

A genuine tramp, if ever there was one.

As he shambled up to the veranda, took off his hat and made a low bow, Lee improved the opportunity to toss him a dime, saying:

"There's a dime for you, my good man; take yourself off now, and don't ever come and bother us again."

"Faix, and who axed ye for yer dirthy wee bit of silver?" cried the man, in a hoarse, rasping voice, which, to the well trainer ears of the New Yorker, indicated that the speaker had been in the habit of indulging in much more liquor than was good for him,

"Sorra a taste I want of it, do ye mind!" he continued, his tones plainly indicating that he was a son of the Emerald Isle.

"What do you want, then?" asked Miss Somerton, sharply, having formed a decidedly bad opinion of the stranger.

"Is it ye that is Miss Somerton?"

"That is my name."

"Long life to ye, ma'am! Shure ye're the leddy that I want to see!" and he made another profound bow.

"Well, sir, you see me now; what do you want?"

"I'm tould ye're looking afther a foreman to wourk the farm for yees."

"No, sir; I do not require any one."

"Shure I was tould ye wanted a foreman!" he exclaimed, in a dogged sort of way.

"I do not, sir; and I surely ought to know, I am satisfied with my present foreman, and haven't any idea of changing," retorted Miss Somerton, annoyed at the persistence of the fellow, and feeling satisfied he had been drinking.

"Oh, well, I'm not proud. If ye don't be afther wanting a foreman I'll wourk as a reg'lar hand; shure I kin do anything. You can't have a likelier bye about the place than meself."

"I do not require any one at all, sir. In fact, I have too many hands now, and am thinking of getting rid of them."

Miss Somerton wondered that Mr. Lee did not interfere and send the fellow off; but the New Yorker, after examining the man closely for a few minutes, had turned his attention to the distant sails upon the ocean, as though the man was not worth troubling oneself about.

"Ah, a leddy like yerself can always make room for another man on sich an illegant place as this. Shure, miss, can't ye spake a wourd for me for ould acquaint'ship, seein' that we kern over in the same ship?" he said, addressing Helena.

That young lady looked amazed, for she did not remember ever seeing the man before.

"Ye disremember me, mebbe?" he added.

"I certainly cannot recall you just now," Helena answered.

"Ye kem over in the City of Chester, the same as meself."

"Yes, I did come in that steamer; but I don't remember meeting you on board of her."

"I was there to the fore, ye kin lay yer life on that. Shure, I kin call ye by name — it was Rarras, or Morras, or something like wan of thim."

"My name is Porras."

"That's it, I knew I knew ye!" exclaimed the fellow, triumphantly.

"There's no place for you here, my man, and you had better retire," Miss Somerton remarked, sternly.

"Shure, I won't stay if yees don't want me to, and I'll take a wee bit of silver, more glory to yees," responded the man, with an injured air, then he picked up the dime and shambled off.

"I don't like the looks of that fellow," Lee remarked, abruptly, after the man had got out of earshot. "It seems to me that there is something wrong about him."

"He has evidently been drinking; but now he's gone, thank goodness!" Miss Somerton cried.

The conversation then turned on other subjects, and shortly afterward Mr. Lee took his departure for the city.

Helena retired to her room that night with her mind full of strange fancies; but she gave little thought to the odd old Irishman, for although she did not remember him, yet she did not doubt that he spoke the truth in regard to crossing the ocean in the same steamer; but Mr. Lee — why did that young gentleman affect her so strangely? Why was it when she thought of him that a presentiment of danger came upon her?

It was very strange.

She had been sitting by the open window meditating, and now arose to prepare to retire. A glass of wine-lemonade upon the table attracted her attention, and her grateful heart beat more quickly at this proof of her protector's thoughtfulness. "She is so kind," she murmured, as she drank the refreshing draught. But hardly had she drained

the glass when a death-like numbness seized upon her —
she tottered forward, and then sunk down senseless.

CHAPTER XXXVI.

THE drug which had been instilled into the lemonade
was so potent that it overpowered the girl's senses almost
immediately; she was helpless before she was aware that
anything was wrong.

How long she remained in such a state she knew not, but
when she began to revive and distinguish objects around
her, she found she was in a narrow apartment, obscured
by gloom, and the sound of working machinery with the
splash of dashing waves came distinctly to her ears.

She was apparently moving, yet the apartment she sat in
was stationary.

But just as her mind had recovered sufficiently to reason in
regard to where she was, and she had come to the conclusion
that she was in a close place, a voice sounded in her ears.

She had moved, and so betrayed to the careful watchfulness
of the person who sat beside her that consciousness was
returning.

"Not yet — not yet," said the voice in tones that she
remembered only too well. "It is too soon; we are not yet at
our journey's end."

And then a strong arm encircled her and a damp sponge,
with its pores filled with some potent, pungent smelling
liquid, was pressed to her nostrils.

The full extent of the horrible situation in which she was placed flashed upon her.

She had been drugged and abducted!

And she was not ignorant, either, in regard to the author of the outrage, for she recognized him by the tones of his voice.

She tried to struggle — to cry out — but the strong arm fettered her as though she was in a vise, and the powerful drug applied to her nostrils quickly stole her senses away.

Again she relapsed into helplessness -- completely in the power of her abductor.

When consciousness returned the scene had changed.

She was in a brilliantly lighted, luxuriantly furnished apartment, reclining in an easy-chair, as comfortable as a couch.

Where was she?

She looked around her, conscious she had been the victim of a terrible outrage, and yet unable to guess why she was attacked; for she had not a foe in the world to her knowledge.

Her eyes fell upon a man seated in a great arm-chair a few paces from her, his eyes fixed with an earnest gaze upon her face.

There was a strange mocking smile upon his features, and as the astonished girl gazed upon him a horrid truth flashed suddenly upon her.

She had recognized him at the first glance.

It was the New York gentleman who had been introduced to her by Miss Somerton only a few hours before.

Then his face had seemed familiar to her, and she had been puzzled to account for it, for she could not remember ever having met him before, but now, like a flash, the problem was solved.

This was the man who so boldly abducted her from the deck of the steamer.

A sickening sensation came over her; again she was helpless in the power of one who, if not a maniac, was a very fiend in human form.

She closed her eyes as if to shut out the horrid sight, and a convulsive shudder shook her frame.

The captain noticed the movement, and he laughed outright. A low, cunning laugh, utterly devoid of merriment, but full of menace.

Again the girl shuddered.

"No need of shutting your eyes," he remarked. "I am here all the same, though you shut me from your sight. You cannot get rid of a disagreeable fact by so simple a process as merely closing your eyes to it."

Our heroine was a brave girl, one full of resolution, yet so intense was the terror inspired by this extraordinary man, she felt as weak and powerless as a puny child.

The feeling that possessed her was akin to the horrible fright which would have seized upon her if in some woodland glade she had stepped suddenly upon a slimy serpent and then beheld the reptile raise its crested head to strike.

This man seemed to her to be more than human. The boldness of his attacks and the success which had attended them astounded her.

From the first she had escaped as though by a miracle, but would Heaven again interpose its mighty arm in her behalf.

She endeavored to collect her thoughts; no easy matter now that she fully understood her position, and besides, her brain was still whirling from the effects of the powerful drug which had been administered to her by the abductor.

With a great effort she endeavored to appear calm, striving not to betray the fear to which she was a prey.

She opened her eyes and looked her captor full in the face.

"Good! that's a brave girl!" he exclaimed. "There's nothing like making the best of a bad bargain, and to boldly confront a danger at once reduces its extent. I think I perceive that you recognize me."

"Yes."

"But you did not when we met in the country."

"No; although I knew your face was familiar, yet I could not remember where I had seen you.'"

"It was strange, for I disguised myself materially when I assumed the *role* of the half-witted Frenchman; but how is it that you recognize me now when your memory did not serve you then?"

"Because you no longer attempt to control your features, you have thrown off the mask, and any one who has ever seen your fiendish smile would never be apt to forget it," she exclaimed.

Again the man laughed, for the speech pleased him.

"You are right," he remarked, "a victim once transfixed by my eyes seldom forgets the experience."

"But what is the meaning of this terrible outrage?" exclaimed the girl, hotly, unable to restrain herself. "How have I ever injured you — what do you intend to do with me? I have nothing — I am nothing — why, then, do you persecute me?"

"Faith, it fairly rains questions!" he cried, with the shrill laugh that so disagreeably affected the girl. "It may not be so easy for me to answer the questions as it is for you to ask them. In the first place, I am not sure that I can give you my reasons. Look in my eyes — do you see anything odd about them?"

"Yes, there is a strange glitter and glare, as if you were not in your right mind," she answered, promptly.

"That is exactly the thought that comes to me, sometimes, and I sit and ponder over it; am I crazy, or am I not? In my actual self — for, as you have doubtless guessed, I lead two lives, and they are almost as widely separated as the poles — I know I am all right, and I challenge any one to point out a blemish; but in the other, when I give my fancy full reign, I am either mad or else a demon; yet if I am mad, like Hamlet, there's method in it.

"I have not sought you just by chance, but through deep design. When my mad fit is on me I am reckless as to the consequences; the wilder and more daring the scheme that comes into my head the better I like it.

"Your life is shrouded in mystery. You came a stranger here to meet strangers, but I stepped in between.

"The fury of the elements tore you from me, but the chapter of accidents again brought us together, and eagerly I snatched at the chance.

"Again you are in my power, and this time I fancy you will not escape until my purpose is accomplished.

"Girl, it is written in the stars that you must become my wife."

She started in horror.

"That surprises you, eh?" he continued. "Well, I suppose it is rather startling, being so entirely unexpected; but that is the way, it is the unexpected that always happens."

"But such a thing will not happen!" she exclaimed, her anger rising at the cool assurance of her captor.

"It will happen within the next month as surely as you are a living, breathing woman. Reflect for a moment upon the position you occupy," he replied, calmly. "You are here in my power, utterly helpless. No one knows that you are here, and your friend in the country will not be apt to trouble herself to search after you, for when she discovers you are missing she will also find that she is minus some valuable trinket. I was careful to arrange this little matter. As it stands, Miss Somerton, in disgust, will look upon you as a snake which, after being warmed to life, turned upon and stung its benefactor."

"Oh, you are a demon!" Helena cried, horrified at this revelation.

"Yes, to those who attempt to cross me in my way. It is necessary for certain purposes that we become man and wife. There isn't anything romantic about the affair. I am not at all in love with you and I don't expect you to profess any affection for me, but you must be my wife, and I haven't any doubt that we will get along just as well as the majority of married folks."

"I will never consent!"

"Oh, yes, you will! I shall tame you into submission. You are as securely a prisoner here as though you were immured in a dungeon a hundred feet beneath the earth's surface. I shall starve you until you consent. Neither food nor water shall pass your lips until your proud spirit is broken. Ten hours' reflection I give you and then come again."

With this Lee quitted the apartment, closing the door carefully behind him. It was fastened by a powerful spring-lock.

CHAPTER XXXVII.

THE apartment into which Lee entered was the one to which we before introduced the reader; the library, where the consultation between the scheming doctor and the traitorous May had taken place. A tray containing a decanter of brandy and some glasses was on the table.

Lee sat down in his favorite seat, a leather cushioned arm-chair, and helped himself to a glass of the potent liquor.

"Aha! that's the stuff," he exclaimed; "that puts new life into a man. I do not exactly understand it, but, somehow, I don't feel as well as I ought to under the circumstances. Everything is progressing as well as I could possibly wish. I have succeeded in all my designs, and unless some evil genius rises to snatch my prize from me my fortune is made. The girl will consent to the marriage in time, and if she does not, I will so weaken her down with drugs — so enfeeble her mind — that when the time for the ceremony arrives she will be but little better than an idiot, and will not have sense enough to resist. All I am afraid of is myself. I am half mad at times; I know it; I am quite conscious when the spell comes on, and then I am a perfect wild beast, hungry for blood and slaughter. But will not the time come at last when the mind will give way and the madness become permanent? That will be an interesting study. Many men are crazy more or less, but few of them are aware of it, as I am, and fewer still capable of calmly waiting and watching its development."

He took another glass of brandy.

"What is the matter with me?" he exclaimed. "I am nervous and ill at ease. Is there some danger impending? That old tramp! that fellow inspired me with fear. If I were not sure that Brand perished beneath the waters of the North River, I should have suspected that the tramp was he in disguise. The man-hunter is dead — and the dead do not return."

Hardly had the words left his lips when from behind a Japanese fire-screen, which stood in a corner of the room, rose the figure of the old tramp, a cocked and leveled revolver in his hand.

"Does not the Brand always rise from its ashes?" he asked, at the same time removing his wig and beard, and displaying the resolute features of the detective.

Lee sunk back in his chair with a convulsive gasp. He realized the situation upon the instant.

He was hunted down.

"Do not attempt to resist," continued Brand, coming from behind the screen. "The house is filled with police: your two confederates are in our hands, and in order to save themselves they have made a clean breast of it. You didn't finish me the other night, as you thought, for as I came to the surface of the water I saw you returning, and I conjectured that you had an idea of making an end of me, and as I wasn't in a good condition for any more fighting, my revolvers being useless from the ducking, I took advantage of the fact that your back was turned to crawl out and hide among the rocks.

"But I lost your trail, though, all the same, and I only struck it again by an accident. I was employed by Anchona to find this girl, Helena, and when I discovered that she was under Miss Somerton's protection I assumed a disguise in order to ascertain exactly how matters stood, and so was lucky enough to stumble upon you, and I recognized you that time, Lee, although you fooled me completely when you were disguised as a woman.

"The game was up then, for I felt sure that you were the man who tried to abduct the girl from the steamer, and I reckoned you would try it again.

"When you carried off the girl in your coach I followed you on horseback, having previously warned the police by telegraph.

"The coach, with the trap-door in the floor, by means of which you were enabled to leave the bodies of your victims wherever you pleased, with little danger of detection, is in our hands.

"The cloak you sometimes wore, which gave you the appearance of a gigantic bird, and so inspired credulous souls with terror, we have also captured, together with sundry valuables, the property of the men so fiendishly slain by you."

"Ha, ha, ha!" laughed Lee, suddenly recovering his composure, "I have played a bold game, haven't I? It was easy enough in my disguises to entrap my victims. They entered the house on one street, met their doom there, then were carried to the stable in the rear on another street, placed in the coach, and their bodies thus easily disposed of.

"Probably you have suspected that at times I am not exactly in my right mind."

"I have, for only a demon or a madman could accomplish such deeds of blood," replied the detective.

"My particular craze, when the fit came on, was to believe I was a vampire, one of those fabulous creatures who live on human blood. I slew my victims, and then I pricked them in the neck with the dagger point, just as if the vampire's teeth had bitten there.

"I have reason for my madness — too — reason to hate the world.

"I was reared as the scion of a wealthy creole family, but when I returned from Europe to claim my estates on the death of my parents, I discovered that I was naught but a penniless beggar, the child of a quadroon slave; the blow drove me mad. I was sent to an asylum, where I was treated in the most cruel manner.

"At last my reason returned to me, and I was discharged cured. From that time I have preyed upon my fellow men as mercilessly as any wild beast.

"When you got upon my track I feared the worst, and so I tried my utmost to kill you. Fate is against me, and to it I yield.

"You have stopped me right at the moment of success. This girl, Helena, is to be the old banker's heiress. I was going to marry her, kill Anchona, and so clutch his fortune. But you will not tang me, though, for I am crazy."

"So reasoned another great criminal, but the law took his life, nevertheless!" exclaimed Brand.

"It will not take mine, for I am already dying. Like the scorpion when driven to bay, I sting myself to death!"

He held up his left hand, upon the little finger of which gleamed a heavy ring.

"This is the poison ring of the ancient Borgias!" he cried wildly. "A slight pressure drives its poisoned fangs into the hand it touches. See! thus do I defy your malice!"

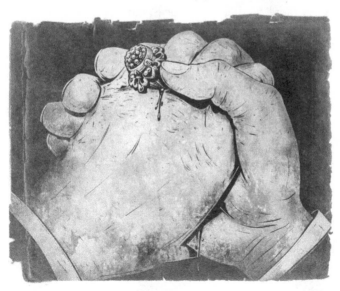

He clasped his hands before the detective could spring forward to prevent it.

Wildly he laughed, and rising brandished his hands in the air, waving the detective away.

Almost immediately the powerful poison took effect.

"I feel it sapping the life within my veins!" he cried. "No scaffold-beam, no hangman's rope for me! Brand, accursed man-hunter, my blood is on your head -- in death I defy thee!"

Lee sunk back in the chair; a few convulsive gasps and the secret slayer was beyond the ken of the law.

He was dead.

* * *

A few more words and our tale is told.

Helena was conducted by Brand to the house of the banker, and there Anchona explained that it was through him that she quitted England.

Then came the story of the marvelous adventures that had befallen the girl since her arrival in the New World, and Brand, thanks to the revelation made to him by the baffled villain, was able to explain the motive which had caused Lee to so persistently prosecute the maiden.

Miss Sornerton's kindness to the unfortunate girl was also made known to Anchona, and the banker was greatly affected.

"A coldness has existed between that lady and myself for over twenty years on your father's account," the banker said. "My unfortunate brother, whose rashness not only wrecked his own life, but also rendered miserable all connected with him.

"Yes, my child, your father was my brother William; Miss Somerton must be summoned, for now I can explain everything."

Brief and sad was the story of William Anchona.

Even while engaged to be married to Miss Somerton, he became infatuated with another woman, married her in secret — was supposed by her brothers to have betrayed her, and they waylaid him. In the struggle one of the brothers was killed by William; and to avoid the consequences of his crime he fled to foreign parts, and there assumed another name, and to the day of his death never dared to return to his native land, or allow any one to know he lived, the banker excepted, for it was he who aided the fugitive to escape.

When Miss Somerton heard this story, she was satisfied that it was the hand of Heaven that had led her to Helena; the love she bore the father had descended to the daughter.

The banker knew naught of the lady whom his brother had married abroad, and fearing that William had again made an unfortunate match, was resolved not to let the child, the issue of the marriage, know of the bright fortune in store for her, until he had ascertained she was worthy of it.

But Helena was a paragon of a woman, as Miss Somerton declared, and the banker soon learned to love her as if she had been his own child.

Blakely, like the worthy, honest fellow that he was, deemed the now wealthy girl a prize too great for him to aspire to gain, but Anchona speedily reassured him on this point.

"You were her steadfast friend when fortune frowned, do not now forsake her now that she is again in the sunshine!" he exclaimed.

Thus encouraged Blakely persevered, and rumor whispers that soon the wedding will take place.

And now, having brought order out of chaos, having solved as terrible a mystery as ever bewildered the police of a great city, having written the career and described the tracking down and death of the most remarkable assassin of modern times, we bring our story to

THE END

This ad for The Vampire was featured in a catalog for Old Cap Collier Library titles. It gives a sensational, but somewhat inaccurate summary of the plot.

AMERICA'S FIRST VAMPIRE NOVEL

AND THE SUPERNATURAL AS ARTIFICE

Gary D. Rhodes and John Edgar Browning

Histories of vampire literature traditionally concentrate on four key texts published in Great Britain in the nineteenth century: John Polidori's novelette, *The Vampyre, A Tale* (1819), James Malcolm Rymer's (or Thomas Peckett Prest's) penny dreadful *Varney the Vampire; or, The Feast of Blood* (1845-47); J. Sheridan Le Fanu's novella *Carmilla* (1872); and Bram Stoker's novel *Dracula* (Constable, 1897). In them are important evolutions and consolidations of the vampire we see in fiction today. Fans of the subject seek out these texts, reading and re-reading them, or at the very least – in the case of *Varney* – memorizing the cover image of the 1853 edition while scanning the voluminous word count (totaling some 666,000 and then some).

Scholarly interest in the subject has led to emphasis on other nineteenth-century works, including stage adaptations of Polidori's tale, among them James Robinson Planché's *The Vampire; or the Bride of the Isles* (1820). Roxana Stuart's *Stage Blood: Vampires of the 19th-Century Stage* (1994), for example, recovers much information on vampire characters in European theater[1]. Nevertheless, further

---

1 Roxana Stuart, *Stage Blood: Vampires of the 19th-Century Stage* (Bowling Green, Ohio: Bowling Green State University Popular Press, 1994).

literary excavations are still necessary. Much remains to be rediscovered, particularly in terms of the United States.

However much attention American scholars have rightly paid to *Varney* and *Carmilla* in the late twentieth and early twenty-first centuries, those two texts made little-to-no impact in nineteenth-century America (though a recent discovery by John Edgar Browning shows that *Carmilla* did at least see serial publication[2]). And while *Dracula* became an immediately popular success,[3] it was not published in the United States until 1899, by which time it had already been translated into Hungarian in 1898 and serialized in a Budapest newspaper, then in English in a Chicago newspaper a year later before the American book release (Doubleday & McClure Co., 1899).[4]

By contrast, American newspapers wrote at length about the publication of *The Vampyre* in 1819. The vampire (or, more ornately, "vampyre") started to appear in American newspapers as early as the eighteenth century, often pejoratively to refer to businessmen, corporations, banks, bankers, landlords, and politicians. Medicinal treatment advertisements also employed the vampire to describe a range of illnesses, like scrofula (a form of tuberculosis). Even science turned to the vampire to identify various species of bat and

---

2 Joseph Sheridan Le Fanu's *Carmilla* (1872) appeared in serial form in *The Sunny South* (Atlanta, GA), beginning in vol. 3, no. 134 (January 12, 1878): 1-2.

3 John Edgar Browning, *Dracula—An Anthology: Critical Reviews and Reactions, 1897-1920* (Edinburgh University Press, 2022).

4 See Simone Berni, *Dracula by Bram Stoker: The Mystery of the Early Editions* (Biblohaus, 2016).

squid. Newspapers were seemingly all too eager to cash in on the vampire's rising popularity with the publication of *The Vampyre*. Despite some negative reviews, the story seems to have been an immediate hit with American readers. Uriah Derick D'Arcy quickly published a "burlesque" entitled, *The Black Vampyre* in New York, the stated aim being to "ridicule" the story.[5] And in what was likely the first performance of a vampire play in the United States, the Pavillion Theatre in New York staged *The Vampyre*, an apparently unauthorized and loose adaptation of the story in July 1819.[6]

The following year, *The Vampire; or the Bride of the Isles* made its New York debut. Versions continued to be staged in America often during the years that followed. As an article in the *New York Literary Journal* noted in 1821, "Since the appearance of the story of the Vampire, the conversation of private parties has frequently turned to the subject, and the discussion has been prolonged and invigorated by the pieces brought at the theatres...."[7]

The next major appearance of the vampire in America came thanks to Dion Boucicault's two-act play *The Phantom*. Originally staged in England as *The Vampire* in 1852, *The*

---

5 Untitled, *The Village Record* (West Chester, Pennsylvania), September 18, 1819, np.

6 The adaptation seems to have been loose given that the play's three main characters as Lord Ruthven, Aubrey, and Pedro, the latter being a character that does not exist (at least by that name) in Polidori's tale.

7 "On Vampires and Vampirism," New Monthly Magazine and Universal Register (London) 14 (1820): 548-52.

Phantom opened in New York in 1856. Unfortunately, *The Phantom* remains conspicuously absent from many modern vampire histories. While *The Phantom* never became as successful as Boucicault's Irish-themed plays, theatres did stage it occasionally after its New York premiere. As late as 1870, a version of it appeared in Galveston, Texas.[8]

All of this history—as well as popular attention paid to Philip Burne-Jones painting *The Vampire* (1897) and Rudyard Kipling's poem of the same name and year—represents a particularized lineage, meaning that some, but not all fictional vampires from Europe arrived on U.S. soil and had varying degrees of success with readers and theatergoers. It is a decidedly American tale, though, one of foreign invasion by vampires. But however much it needs to be investigated, it is only part of the story of American vampires in the nineteenth century.

The key missing link in previous histories is America's first vampire novel. Published in 1885, *The Vampire; or, Detective Brand's Greatest Case* has languished in obscurity, cited only briefly in a few recent texts.[9] And yet it may have been the

---

8 Untitled, *Flake's Bulletin,* January 22, 1870, np.

9 *The Vampire; or, Detective Brand's Greatest Case* is mentioned in Gary D. Rhodes, "The First Vampire Films in America," *Palgrave Communications* 3, article no. 51 (2017): https://doi.org/10.1057/s41599-017-0043-y; Gary D. Rhodes, *The Birth of the American Horror Film* (Edinburgh: Edinburgh University Press, 2018), 31; and Kevin Dodd, "'Blood Suckers Most Cruel': The Vampire and the Bat In and Before Dracula," *Athens Journal of Humanities and Arts 6,* no. 2 (2019): 107-32.

most widely read vampire novel in America prior to the publication of Stoker's *Dracula*.

Written anonymously, *The Vampire; or, Detective Brand's Greatest Case* was published as a "dime novel." Dime novels—which were really novellas or "novelettes"— featured tales of Native Americans, western heroes and outlaws, the American Civil War, detectives, and/or horror. During the late nineteenth century, the term "dime novel" had become used generically to describe much paperback fiction, regardless of the cover price. J. Randolph Cox writes:

> In the beginning, the term 'dime novel' was a brand name. *Beadle's Dime Novels* (1860-1874) was a series of paper-covered booklets, published at regular intervals and numbered in sequence. For 14 years, a new title was issued by the publishers, Beadle and Adams, every two weeks or so, 321 in all.
>
> … Imitation being a good way to make money, as well as the sincerest form of flattery, it wasn't long before other publishers issued their own variations on the Beadle dime novel theme. In 1863, a former employee of Erastus Beadle, George P. Munro, became his chief competitor by issuing a series called *Munro's Ten Cent Novels*.[10]

---

10 J. Randolph Cox, *The Dime Novel Companion: A Source Book* (Westport, Connecticut: Greenwood Press, 2000), xii-xiv.

Munro's brother, Norman L. Munro, ran his own dime novel company, which published *The Vampire; or, Detective Brand's Greatest Case* on September 14, 1885 as part of the "Old Cap Collier Library."

Gary Hoppenstand writes, "there has always existed a Bermuda Triangle in detective fiction, a vacuum, if you will, that has absorbed an entire archetype for over a hundred years."[11] Reasons range from the limited availability of dime novels for study as well as prejudice against the form. Indeed, Kevin Dodd describes *The Vampire; or, Detective Brand's Greatest Case* as an "adolescent" novel, which is true insofar as dime novels largely targeted young men (even though the reading demographic for them may well have been larger).[12] However, the word "adolescent" is misleading insofar as indicating the type of language and prose style it utilizes. Here is not a book solely for children, in other words, not by any means.

Hoppenstand and others have attributed *The Vampire; or, Detective Brand's Greatest Case* to Hawley Smart, but there is no compelling reason to believe he is the actual author. More important than the writer's name, though, is what he or she wrote, as the dime novel is quite different than its predecessors in vampire fiction. The book's key revelation—that the "supernatural" vampire is merely an

---

11 Gary Hoppenstand, "Introduction: The Missing Detective," in *The Dime Novel Detective,* ed. Gary Hoppenstand (Bowling Green, Ohio: Bowling Green University Popular Press, 1982), 3.

12 Dodd, "'Blood Suckers Most Cruel'," 119.

insane, bloodthirsty villain making puncture marks on his victims' throats—places it at the forefront of an entirely new type of vampire fiction—one that would later thrive in such films as *London after Midnight* (Tod Browning, 1927), *Mark of the Vampire* (Tod Browning, 1935), and—most especially—*Martin* (George Romero, 1978).

American Horror Before 1885

The Vampire; or, Detective Brand's Greatest Case represented an entirely new kind of vampire fiction when it was published. But it was also part of a larger continuum, one in which horror themes in American literature were treated in two particular respects. Of these, one particular focus was on real-life horrors. As Daniel A. Cohen has noted, American publications on murder and capital punishment date to the first half of the eighteenth century, when "gallows broadsides" published the dying words of the condemned, as well as details of their crimes. Later, in the early decades of the nineteenth century, murder trial reports in newspapers became popular, as did biographies of criminals.[13]

As Karen Halttunen indicates in *Murder Most Foul: The Killer and the American Imagination* (1998), the subject of

---

13 Daniel A. Cohen, "Blood Will Out: Sensationalism, Horror, and the Roots of American Crime Literature," in *Mortal Remains: Death in Early America,* ed. Nancy Isenberg and Andrew Burstein (Philadelphia: University of Pennsylvania Press, 2003), 54.

murder in popular fiction and nonfiction literature grew dramatically after the 1820s, the result of many causes, among them an escalation in literacy rates.[14] Reading became common, with murder helping to lead the charge. Halttunen observes:

> This literature did not simply report 'intense excitement'; it actively sought to stimulate it, intentionally sending a 'thrill of horror' to readers' hearts... Most important, murder literature after 1800 focused overwhelmingly on images of the body in pain and death. The primary technique of sensationalism was body-horror, the effort to arouse the readers' repugnance (and excitement) in the face of the physiological realities of violent death.[15]

Halttunnen explains further that "Reading horror literature thus helped reinforce the rising levels of repression demanded by the growing humanitarian sanctions against violent impulses and actions."[16]

The other main trajectory of American horror was to invoke the supernatural only to rationalize it. Most commonly, American writers chose to expose the "supernatural" as being the product of all-too-human

---

14 Halttunen, *Murder Most Foul*, 36, 69.

15 Halttunen, *Murder Most Foul*, 73.

16 Halttunen, *Murder Most Foul*, 82.

trickery. The Enlightenment won over Old World superstitions. And then there was the human mind, capable of playing tricks on oneself or others. America's first novelist Charles Brockden Brown explored these possibilities in *Wieland, or The Transformation* (1798). In this novel, Brown describes a family living in a mansion near Philadelphia. The character Theodore Wieland slaughters his relatives because he believes God has told him to do so. However, the voice he hears is apparently that of the all-too-human Carwin, a "biloquist" (ventriloquist). Then, in William Austin's *The Man with the Cloaks: A Vermont Legend* (1836), the narrator announces, "There was nothing supernatural in this; the body is often the plaything of the mind." The mental state of first-person narrators also became a particularly successful mechanism for writing about the supernatural while still explaining it. The rational largely triumphed during the nineteenth century, so much so that, in 1913, a critic made the following plea:

> Wanted – a ghost story: a romance in which the spectre is a real one. ... The advertiser thus requests because she is weary of the ghost that ultimately proves to be an escaped maniac, a wandering baboon, or a six-year-old masquerading in her aunt's dress.[17]

17 M. H. Menaugh, "Bookish Chats, No. IX–The Ghost in Fiction," *Colman's Rural World,* January 16, 1913, 10.

Is there a headless horseman in Sleepy Hollow, or is it merely Brom Bones playing a joke on poor Ichabod Crane? Had the title character of Hawthorne's *Young Goodman Brown* (1835) fallen asleep and merely dreamed of witches? Be it so, if you will. Are there ghosts in Henry James' *The Turn of the Screw* (1898), or is the problem a deluded mind of the type Poe so regularly examined?

To be sure, there are exceptions to these two approaches to American horror, but the numbers do not lie. To detail murder, and to broach the supernatural without verifying it, or dismiss it outright: here is where most American texts situated themselves prior to 1885. *The Vampire; or, Detective Brand's Greatest Case* drew upon these traditions, both of which converge within its pages.

DETECTIVE BRAND'S GREATEST CASE

The story begins on a spring day. It is early evening, and the weather mild, when a policeman walking the city streets discovers a murder victim, and something else, afar in the distance, which "froze him with horror": the figure of a man "framed against the moon," resembling in that frightful moment "a huge bird...attired entirely in black." Prior to the incident, dead bodies had been appearing on the streets of New York with puncture wounds on their necks. "Gotham was puzzled," and:

> The best detectives were at a loss, and candidly confessed their confusion. A [series]

of mysterious deaths and disappearances had called forth the best talent of the metropolitan detective force, but as yet no substantial clew to the perpetrator of the awful murders, and mysterious disappearances, both believed to be the work of the same inhuman fiend, had been obtained. Murders were common enough in New York, but there was an unusual factor in these of which we write, and it was something so ghoulish, so horrible, so unnatural, that even the tried offices of the force spoke of the matter with whispering voices, and sometimes with a shudder of superstitious horror that could not be repressed.[18]

During the first chapters, a clever detective named Brace chases the culprit, his disguises capable of fooling men assigned to work with him, men who were "all his own brothers." But Brace is still not up to the task. In Chapter XI, his corpse is discovered. An "examination revealed that he had perished from a stab wound piercing the heart, and on the neck, under the left ear, were the two mysterious marks which had also appeared on the bodies of the other victims."[19] And so the arrival of the "keen" Detective

18 Anon, *The Vampire; or, Detective Brand's Greatest Case* (Old Cap Collier Library Series) (New York: Norman L. Munro, Publisher) 2, no. 161 (September 15, 1885): 11.

19 Anon, *The Vampire*, 78.

Carlton Brand becomes necessary. He works for himself, not the police. He is a

> …man possessed of wonderful physical power, undaunted courage, and a face so mobile it was capable of the most astonishing changes, coupled with the instinct of a bloodhound, a more terrible man-catcher never got upon a rascal's track.[20]

Upon learning of Brace's death and the details of the case, Brand explains to the police chief:

> The money is welcome enough, of course, although I am tolerably well provided, but I would undertake the work all the same if there wasn't a dollar up, for this mysterious assassin is no common stabber, and it is these superhuman villains that I delight to track. I believe I ought to have been born a bloodhound, for I take a fierce delight when I can get upon the track of such a magnificent rascal. There is no pleasure hunting down your common vulgar scoundrel; that is, not for a man like myself. If I cannot chase a big game, I prefer to remain idle.[21]

20 Anon, *The Vampire*, 82.

21 Anon, *The Vampire*, 86.

In some respects, Brand exemplifies what Gary Hoppenstand calls the "archetypal Avenger Detective" of dime novels. He works "outside traditional law-enforcement agencies," he "is a man of great wealth," he "is a master of disguise," and he "possesses great strength, superb training and determination, coupled with courage."[22]

Brand is himself a master of disguise, not only of his face, but also of his voice, affecting different accents as needed. But initially he couldn't work on this case. He has been out of America for some time, and "the hot sun of the tropics had bronzed his complexion." He grows his moustache longer and also sports a "small chin-piece, after the foreign fashion."

Brand is also an "old opium-eater." He explains, "Years ago, when trouble nearly drove me crazy, I found relief in that lethe-producing drug, and [became] so used to it that I could take, without harm, a quantity large enough to almost kill a dozen men...." In so many respects, then, Brand is prescient of Conan Doyle's Sherlock Holmes, who would not appear in print for another two years. And,

---

22 Hoppenstand, "Introduction," 4. Hoppenstand notes that the "Avenger Detective" first appeared in the early 1880s and continued into the 1920s. Detective Brand does not exemplify four of the eight qualities that Hoppenstand attributes to the archetype, perhaps because of his appearance so early in its formation. For example, Brand does use "iconic weaponry (most always a gun)," but he does not "combat crime with a dedicated group of assistants," he does not "maintain a sanctum sanctorum for his personal use," and he is not "strongly nationalistic."

although loosely hinted at in Holmes's inaugural appearance in *A Study in Scarlet* (1887), his drug use did not become apparent until Doyle's second novel, *The Sign of the Four* (1890).[23]

An Irish policeman is the first in the narrative to witness the vampire, "a figure strange enough to startle almost anyone, as it appeared, framed against the moon." "Holy Moses! Is it a man or a divil," he cries in language that attempts to mimic his brogue.[24] The novel then explains:

> It is no wonder that he asked the question,
> for at a distance the figure, though evidently
> that of a man, bore a striking resemblance to
> a huge bird, being attired entirely in black,
> wearing a long, old-fashioned circular cloak,
> and just as the officer caught sight of the man,
> he raised and stretched out his arms, and the
> cloak being thus extended, looked exactly like
> a pair of huge wings, and as the man wore, too,
> a small, soft hat, pulled in chapeau fashion
> down over his eyes, so that it came to a point

23 For further commentary, see, for example, D.N. Pearce, "Sherlock Holmes, Conan Doyle and Cocaine," *Journal of the History of the Neurosciences* 3, no. 4 (1994): 227-32; or Kevin R. Loughlin, "It's elementary: the addictions of Sherlock Holmes," *Hektoen International Journal* (Summer 2019): https://hekint.org/2019/09/05/its-elementary-the-addictions-of-sherlock-holmes/.

24 Anon, *The Vampire*, 14.

in front, it gave his head the appearance of a bird of prey.[25]

His black cloak inspires "credulous souls with terror." Could the author have known of the serialized penny dreadful *Varney the Vampire* (1845-47), whose title character wore a black cloak? Not likely, since it was never published in the United States. Perhaps, if the author was indeed American, he was aware of the "black plume and cloak" worn by the title character in Boucicault's *The Vampire* (1852), which was staged with much success in America beginning in 1856 under the title *The Phantom*. More likely still, it was an offshoot of the ever-growing conflation between the supernatural vampire and the (relatively harmless) vampire bat. Indeed, the figure of the "winged vampire" played a prominent role in politicized periodical illustrations, or as the occasional American literary trope (see, for example, "Haidoni and the Vampyres" in A.E.P. Searling's *The Land of Rip Van Winkle* [1884]). Aided by Polidori's *The Vampyre* and the American press, this conflation helped to fan the modern conception of the vampire as sporting fangs. (Indeed, the vampire, or "revenant," of European folklore, on which the vampire of fiction is based, lacked fangs entirely, so whereas the European vampire lent the vampire bat its name, the vampire bat in turn almost assuredly lent the vampire of fiction its fangs.)

25 Anon, *The Vampire*, 14.

As for the murderer, he drives a dagger into the heart of his victims. But he also leaves two puncture marks on their necks, a sign of the vampire. An "old seaman" provides insight for the uninitiated:

> I heered tell on a vampire once down in the Isle of Java.... It was nigh onto twenty years ago, and his hyar thing used for to light onto a sleeping man, w'ot was foolish enough fur to camp out in the woods, fan him with his wings so as fur to keep him from waking, and suck his blood at the same time. I never see'd any of the things, tho' I've heered plenty of yarns 'bout them, but I allers reckoned it was a kind of bird.[26]

Another character explains, "suppose there was a girl of twenty years old, and whose natural term of life would be forty, that is if the vampire did not cut it short." He continues, "By killing her and drinking her blood the vampire added the twenty years of her life to his own...."[27]

In an effort to dig into the underworld and uncover the vampire, Detective Brand initially plays the role of a wealthy foreigner who has come to New York for "amusement."[28] Then he moves further into the "nether world" of Gotham,

26 Anon, *The Vampire*, 45.

27 Anon, *The Vampire*, 46.

28 Anon, *The Vampire*, 109.

disguising himself to see all those sights "found after dark": "The Bon Ton Club the place was called, and those who were not in the secret supposed it to be a clubhouse pure and simple, while in reality it was nothing but a regular gambling hell."[29] During his search, Brand encounters a woman who slips a drug into his drink:

> The woman was quick to discover that though the drug had worked to a charm upon the hotel official, rendering him completely insensible to all that was passing around, yet Brand, although deprived of muscular power, was yet conscious of what was going on.
>
> The woman, who had also sunk back into an easy-chair after drinking, now rose to her feet, with the look of a demon on her face.[30]

Surprised at Brand's resilience, this woman nevertheless knows who he is, and announces that, even if he has been close to death "a hundred times," he has never been nearer his fate. She confesses to being the vampire, and removes a diamond cross from her "lustrous, jet-black hair." Its pin is a dagger, "only a little larger round than an ordinary knitting-needle."[31] Her eyes then "glow with an unnatural light" as she brandishes the weapon in front of Brand:

29 Anon, *The Vampire*, 194.

30 Anon, *The Vampire*, 115.

31 Anon, *The Vampire*, 119.

It is a toy, and yet it has drunk the heart's blood
of many a strong man, and hurled him before
his time into the cold, damp gravel … And
now, Carlton Brand, it is your turn, and after
you, this miserable fool [the hotel official],
although he is barely worth the killing, but I
crave blood – I cannot have too much of it; if
I cannot get plunder, I can, at least, slake my
thirst for gore![32]

But Brand has only pretended to suffer the effects of
the drug. He captures the "infernal vixen," only for her to
escape. No matter: she was "nothing but a plant," or so he
believes, to throw the great detective "off the scent" of the
real culprit.[33]

The vampire is indeed male, here disguised as a woman.
He is tall and slender, and his name is "Mr. Lee." He
purports to have been the best swordsman in his class at
Heidelberg; and, he also claims to be "French Italian."[34]
He affects different accents and is seen with both short and
long hair. He is a "creature of the lost soul who reigns in the
realm of darkness," possessing the "eyes of a fiend," and is
variously referred to as a "devil" and a "demon."[35] He also
has a "demoniac laugh."

---

32 Anon, *The Vampire,* 120.

33 Anon, *The Vampire,* 144.

34 Anon, *The Vampire,* 24, 201.

35 Anon, *The Vampire,* 42-43, 73.

And he develops an abiding fascination for the "reserved" and "lady-like" Helena Porrus. When the two first meet on a boat, he briefly tries to charm her before throwing his arms around her and applying a sponge to her nose. After having drugged her, he plans to glut himself on her blood, as he makes evident:

> [The vampire] is not a fable; such things do exist as you will find to your cost before this night is over; the old life-current ebbs freely in the veins, and a new supply is needed – fresh, young blood. You should live thirty – forty years yet, but you will die to-night, and the years of your life will go to enrich another![36]

But the two become separated. Efforts to save her converge with a storm at sea:

> The stranger, who had been hurled head fore-most into the water, soon rose to the surface, and despite the fact that he was sadly encumbered by the heavy cloak which he wore, struck out with lusty strokes for the overturned boat. A vivid flash of lightning just at this moment lit up the vast expanse of the water, and the girl, who had risen to the surface about the same time, caught sight of

---

36 Anon, *The Vampire*, 75.

her perpetrator, and, as she did not lose her presence of mind in this dread extremity, Helena understood that he was trying to reach the boat, but as she was totally ignorant of the swimmer's art, she could not hope to follow his example.

In her desperation she struck out wildly with her hands to keep from sinking beneath the surface of the wave. She was in the rear of the swimmer so that he did not perceive her.

…The lightning had died away and utter darkness reigned.[37]

Following her prayer, Helena survives not only the treacherous waters, but also a suspicious couple who try to "help" her.

In language that anticipates Stoker's word "lizard" to describe Dracula's movements, the author compares Helena's fear of the vampire to an encounter with "slimy serpent" or "reptile." And the two meet once more. "Again you are in my power," the vampire declares, "and this time I fancy you will not escape until my purpose is accomplished." He means for Helena to become his wife, explaining:

> It is necessary for certain purposes that we become man and wife. There isn't anything romantic about the affair. I am not at all in

37 Anon, *The Vampire,* 89.

> love with you, and I don't expect you to profess
> any affection for me, but you must be my wife,
> and I haven't any doubt that we will get along
> just as well as the majority of married folks.[38]

He is convinced that she will eventually submit, even if it requires him to "enfeeble her mind" with drugs.

But that is not to be. Detective Brand and the vampire meet once again, having weeks earlier fought a sword duel at the exact spot where "Alexander Hamilton fell by the hand of Aaron Burr." By this point, the author has created intriguing parallels between hero and villain. Both men rely on disguises and travel incognito. And the vampire has referred to Brand, ironically, as "blood-thirsty" and as a "demon." Once captured, Lee, the "vampire," admits the truth, explaining to Brand:

> My particular craze, when the fit came on,
> was to believe I was a vampire, one of those
> fabulous creatures who live on human blood.
> I slew my victims, and then I pricked them in
> the neck with the dagger point, just as if the
> vampire's teeth had bitten there.[39]

His madness stems from the fact he returned from Europe to find his inheritance taken from him (due, he learns, to

---

38 Anon, *The Vampire*, 232.

39 Anon, *The Vampire*, 236.

his being the adopted child of a quadroon, or one-quarter, black slave). Now a "penniless beggar" of apparently tainted blood, the "blow" drives him mad. And so he was sentenced to an asylum, treated there in the "most cruel manner," he explains. Once released, he "preyed upon [his] fellow men as mercilessly as any wild beast."[40]

Lee is nothing if not consistent. The so-called vampire's madness has surfaced in the story even prior to his admission that he is no supernatural creature:

> All I am afraid of is myself. I am half mad at times; I know it; I am quite conscious when the spell comes on, and then I am a perfect wild beast, hungry for blood and slaughter. But will not the time come at last when the mind will give way and the madness become permanent? That will be an interesting study. Many men are crazy, more or less, but few of them are aware of it, and fewer still capable of calmly waiting and watching its development.[41]

However insane he is at times, though, the "vampire" has prepared for his own demise. He wears a ring of the Borgias, using it to inject poison into himself. "I feel [the poison] sapping the life within my veins," he declares.

---

40 Anon, *The Vampire*, 236.

41 Anon, *The Vampire*, 234.

Continuing, "No scaffold-beam, no hangman's rope for me! Brand, accursed man hunter, my blood is on your head – in death I defy thee!" he utters before his death.[42]

CONCLUSION

"There was nothing supernatural in this. The body is often the plaything of the mind."

—William Austin, "The Man with the Cloaks: A Vermont Legend" (1836)[43]

Rationalizing the supernatural as human artifice, of which Austin speaks above, helped to bridge the transition from the American Gothic of the nineteenth century to American Realism. In doing so, it kept horror literature vibrant and varied through employing a myriad of genres, characters, and settings, generally relying "not on the supernatural, but instead on such subjects as pseudo-science, otherness, and—perhaps most popular of all—murder."[44] Likewise, racial (and even to some extent, 'gendered') otherness augmented the murder plot in *The Vampire; or, Detective Brand's Greatest Case*.

---

42 Anon, *The Vampire*, 238.

43 William Austin, "The Man with the Cloaks: A Vermont Legend," *The American Monthly Magazine* 6, no. 5 (January 1836): 332.

44 Rhodes, *The Birth of the American Horror Film*, 21-22.

The popularity of dime novels continued right through the early twentieth century, and while some would occasionally invoke the unexplained supernatural, most relied upon the horror *vérité* of murder, mystery, and human butchery. By World War I, the rational had firmly supplanted the supernatural. With the advent of talkies, preference for human monsters over the supernatural would come to dominate the cinema as well. Even though supernatural fiends like Dracula, Frankenstein's Monster, and the Mummy helped jumpstart Classical Hollywood horror in the 1930s, the majority of genre productions in the thirties and forties privileged the mad scientist, just as the seventies and eighties would herald the all-too-human murderer of the Slasher subgenre. In the end, although no more Detective Brand novels would see publication, the realism and plot devices of *The Vampire; or, Detective Brand's Greatest Case* anticipate several evolutionary milestones in horror cinema, and that's worth a supernatural monster or two any day.

9 781736 386644